Sheldon's only sibling, Blake, has vanished. Sheldon is re-lieved when Blake finally calls, but Blake refuses to explain what he got himself into. That means Sheldon has to get in-volved before Blake gets in even more trouble — even if it ends badly.

And it does.

As a dragon, Morven doesn't trust humans, not even his best friend's lover, Blake. But now Blake needs help to save his brother, and Morven can't say no. He doesn't expect anything but a rescue mission, and he certainly doesn't expect Sheldon.

Sheldon is terrified of the dragons who rescue him, but at least he's with his brother. Who lives with dragons. Can Sheldon wrap his head around it? It's an entirely new world. Ulti-mately, Sheldon will have to choose whether to stay with the dragon shifter who steals his heart or go home to his abusive parents and his empty apartment.

It would be an easy choice if he didn't have dragons trying to kill him.

Green Way Out
Copyright © 2020 Catherine Lievens
ISBN: 978-1-4874-3134-1
Cover art by Angela Waters

Published by eXtasy Books Inc or
Devine Destinies, an imprint of eXtasy Books Inc

Look for us online at:
www.eXtasybooks.com or www.devinedestinies.com

Green Way Out
Ogorth Clan 2

By

Catherine Lievens

CHAPTER ONE

Sheldon couldn't focus. God knew he'd tried. He didn't love his job, but he was proud of the fact that he was good at it, at least usually. Right now, though, the images on the screen were blurry, and he couldn't stop thinking about his brother.

He hadn't heard from Blake in a while, and he was getting worried. He'd told his brother he shouldn't be working at that bar, but Blake hadn't listened. Sheldon couldn't blame him entirely for that, either. Blake needed the money, just like everyone else, and he'd worked whatever job he could find. And now, he was gone, and Sheldon didn't know what to do.

He opened his desk drawer and took his cell phone out. He didn't usually make personal phone calls at work, but he knew his bosses wouldn't care. If it helped him focus better, he was ready to do just about anything.

But when he tried calling, the phone was off.

It didn't even ring, and it made Sheldon even more worried instead of reassuring him and enabling him to focus on what he was doing. What was he supposed to do now? He wanted to find Blake, but he didn't know where to start. Apart from calling, there was no way for him to know where his brother was or if anything had happened to him. He had to find a way, though. His family might not care about Blake anymore, but he did, and he wouldn't let his brother disappear without doing everything he could to find him.

His cell phone rang in his hand, startling him. His heart raced as he looked at the screen, hoping against all odds that it was Blake.

1

It wasn't. It was his mother, and he didn't want to answer. He let the call end, but before he could put his phone back into the drawer, a text arrived. He opened it, glad his parents didn't know how to use the most popular messaging apps. This way, they wouldn't know he'd seen the message and wasn't answering.

Remember to come over tonight.

That was it. It didn't explain why, but Sheldon didn't want to go. He also was pretty sure he couldn't have remembered, because he'd never heard about this before. He tried to spend as little time as possible with his parents and the rest of his family, but he wasn't free of them, unlike Blake.

He winced. He knew that Blake wasn't free of their family because he wanted to be. But he'd come out to their parents, and they'd kicked him out, declaring they only had one son. That son was Sheldon, and he couldn't abandon his parents, no matter how much he wanted to. He knew they would freak out if they found out he wasn't straight, which was why he'd never said anything. That was one more thing he was jealous of Blake for.

Blake didn't have their family anymore, but he was *free*. He didn't have to work with their expectations, to put up a brave front, to listen to them rant. If they had it their way, Blake and Sheldon would be treated like half-humans just because they liked men. It wasn't fair, but then, there was no fairness in life. Blake might be sad he'd lost their family, and he might have to do whatever job he could find, but that was the point. He could do whatever he wanted.

Sheldon couldn't.

Another text arrived. *We're expecting you at five PM.*

Sheldon sighed. There was no getting out of this, no matter what his parents wanted.

He put his phone back into the drawer, closed it, then turned his attention back to the computer screen. He swallowed, because even though he'd done what he could, his brother was still at the back of his mind.

Where was Blake? What was happening to him? Why was his phone off, and why wasn't he answering?

Sheldon had answers to none of those questions, and he didn't know how to get them. He wanted someone to talk to about Blake, but he knew better than to go to their parents. They acted as if Blake had never existed, and Sheldon went along with it. Some days, he wished he could just leave them behind the way Blake had, even though his brother hadn't wanted it. He had responsibilities, though. If their parents lost Sheldon, too, they would be alone. Sheldon would never forgive himself for abandoning them.

He wasn't sure he could forgive himself for abandoning Blake, yet he was.

He sighed and forced himself to focus on his work. Obsessing over Blake or their parents wouldn't help, and Sheldon needed his job. He couldn't afford to lose it, which meant that he had to put his worries away. Then, once the workday was over, he could think about his brother.

The problem was that the thoughts were always the same. He didn't know what had happened to Blake, and he needed to find out. He dreaded it as much as he wanted it, though.

"Make sure the Denali clan isn't planning anything. Check with our spies and give me the report," Morven ordered.

Octavia nodded and turned around to leave. Morven wished he could go with her, but even though he was still technically part of their team, he had more important things to do.

Damn Orran.

Morven sighed. He couldn't berate his best friend for agreeing to become a tutor to Blue, the queen's son. If Morven had had the chance, he probably would have accepted, too.

Or maybe not. He was a guard and a protector at heart. He wanted to continue doing that for the clan, although he wished he wasn't in charge of the clan's security. It was too many responsibilities for him, but he hadn't exactly had a choice. He couldn't say no to the queen when she'd asked him if he wanted to take Orran's place as head of security.

Even though he hadn't.

Morven wished he could go back to the times when he didn't have responsibilities, but he needed to focus on what he could actually do, since that wasn't possible. Octavia and the rest of the team had their orders. Now Morven had to move on to the next part of his day.

He looked down at his list and grimaced. He didn't like berating the guards for not doing their jobs—especially when they were as young as this one was—but if he didn't, they would never learn. He tapped his fingertips onto the piece of paper, sighed heavily, and looked up. He nodded at the guard standing by the door, and the guard opened it. He stepped outside, gesturing at someone, and when he came back in, the young guard Morven had to talk to followed him.

He looked nervous. Morven was pretty sure he expected Morven to burn him to a crisp, and he almost rolled his eyes. Instead, he kept his expression neutral. "You know why you're here?" he asked.

The guard licked his lips. He couldn't seem to manage to look Morven in the eyes, which was just as well. "Because I wasn't at my post when I should have been."

"Exactly. What do you have to say for yourself?"

"I didn't do it on purpose."

Morven arched a brow because he was pretty sure that wasn't the truth. He didn't even have to say anything before the guard continued.

"I swear, I'm not lying."

"Leaving your post seems to have been done on purpose.

What do you mean?"

"A friend came by. He had too much to drink, and I had to take him back to his room. I didn't want him to get hurt."

Morven felt for that. He'd helped friends to their rooms more than once after they drank too much, and he would do it again if he had to. Still, it wasn't a good excuse. "The clan's safety relies on you and the other guards. What do you think would have happened if a dragon from another clan had noticed you weren't there and had used the opening to sneak in?"

The guard's lower lip trembled, and Morven prayed he wasn't about to cry. "I'm sorry," the guard said.

"Being sorry isn't enough. This is your first warning, and there won't be a second one. When you're working, you're working, and nothing else. Do you understand?"

The guard nodded. "I promise it won't happen again."

"See that it doesn't. This is your second chance, and the last one." Morven softened his tone. "We need young guards like you. The clan relies on you, and it wouldn't exist without you. Be proud of the job you do. Do it well. It's all the queen asks from you. If you don't want to be a guard anymore, that's perfectly fine, but you'd have to step down and be replaced. If you haven't changed your mind, do your job well."

The guard nodded again, and Morven stared at him until he realized he needed to leave. He stumbled on his own feet, and Morven had to bite his lower lip not to smile.

Sometimes, he felt more like a babysitter than the head of security. Some of those guards were awfully young, which reminded him of when he and Orran were younger. They'd been childhood friends, and it had been natural for both of them to become guards. Together, they'd climbed the ranks until Orran had become head of security and Morven had led his own team.

And now Orran was a tutor, and Morven had taken his

place.

The door closed behind the guard, and Morven relaxed. It was the last person he had to see this morning, so he had a little time to himself before the afternoon meetings started. Orran had often told him that being head of security wasn't what he'd expected, and now, he understood what it meant. There was a lot less action than he'd thought, and a lot more paperwork and meetings.

Morven left his office through a secondary exit. He didn't want to have to deal with the guards standing outside the main door. They were supposed to follow him when he went around the palace, but he'd done without them all his life, and that wasn't going to change now. He suspected the queen wouldn't be happy with him if she found out, but this was one thing he wasn't willing to compromise on.

He could defend himself if he needed to, and he doubted he would. The palace was safe and guarded, and no outside dragon could come in unless they were invited.

The feeling of sneaking away made him feel a tiny spark of elation. For now, he could stop being head of security and just be Morven, who was looking for his best friend. It would be faster if he shifted, but also more conspicuous, so he stuck to his human form.

That elation disappeared when he knocked on the door to Orran's quarters and Blake was the one who opened.

Morven didn't know what to think of Blake. He was human, and he looked so different. He also thought differently than dragons, and Morven didn't understand why Orran was with him. He realized that the two of them had gone through a lot together, but still. Morven thought they were too different. Orran was a dragon, while Blake was human. He hadn't even known that dragons were shifters until he'd met Orran. Now he was in love with one, and it didn't seem to faze him.

Morven couldn't imagine himself with a human. He'd

never seen Blake without clothes, but he knew humans were very different from dragons. Did Orran really find it attractive?

"Did you want anything?" Blake asked.

Morven nodded. "Is Orran in?"

Blake stepped aside. "He is. Come in."

Morven obeyed. It wasn't just that he didn't understand what Orran saw in Blake. He also didn't understand why the queen had not only agreed to have Blake stay, but also made him a tutor. It was unheard of, but then, it was unheard of to have any human living with dragons. There were grumbles from dragons who weren't happy with her decision, but so far, everything was under control. Morven hoped things would stay that way, but the queen might have to rethink her offer if they didn't.

"Orran?" Blake called out. "Morven is here to see you." He moved toward the nest he and Orran shared.

Morven looked away. He hadn't had a problem being in these rooms before. He'd spent a lot of time here when he and Orran had both been alone, but Orran wasn't anymore. Morven supposed the same would have happened if Orran had been with a dragon, though. Their lives were changing, and they weren't the young guards they'd once been anymore.

Orran emerged from the nest in his human form. Morven had expected it, which was one of the reasons he hadn't shifted into his dragon form when he'd left his office. Orran was spending a lot of time in his human form, which made sense, since he was with a human.

Orran turned to smile at Morven, but Morven didn't miss the way he held his hand out to Blake. Blake took it and raised it to his mouth, kissing the back of it.

Morven forced himself to focus on Orran and not on what Blake was doing. He might not understand why Orran was with Blake, but he couldn't deny they loved each other. It was obvious to anyone with eyes, and luckily, Morven had two of those.

It didn't matter that Blake was human. Morven couldn't say he'd ever wanted to be with one, but it was what *Orran* wanted, and as long as he was happy, Morven wasn't going to say anything about it.

"I wasn't expecting you," Orran said as he moved toward Morven.

"I didn't expect to come by, either. I just wanted to whine."

Orran laughed. "The job is already getting to you?"

"I just had to yell at a guard because he left his post when he shouldn't have. Can you imagine that? He thought his friend being drunk was more important than the clan's safety."

Orran shook his head. "I'm not surprised. He's young?"

"He is. Is this ever going to become easier?"

"I'm afraid not. But it's your job now, and you have to learn to deal with it."

Morven couldn't say he was looking forward to that.

"Why didn't you call a plumber?" Sheldon asked from under the sink.

"Why should I call a plumber?" his father asked.

Sheldon sighed. "Maybe because I have no idea what I'm doing? I'm not a plumber. I work with computers. I don't know how to fix your leak."

"Why did you come, then?"

Sheldon straightened, almost hitting his head on the edge of the counter. "I didn't know this was what you needed. The text only said that I had to remember to come by, not why I had to."

Sheldon's father huffed. "I don't have the money to pay a

plumber."

Sheldon knew that was a lie. His parents had plenty of money, but they were too cheap to use it. They hoarded it and used Sheldon instead. The problem was that Sheldon had no idea how to fix the leak, and he wasn't sure his father understood that. "You still need to call one. I don't know how to help you."

"Are you going to pay for it?"

Sheldon wanted to say no, but he already knew how this was going to end. "Of course."

His father's smile was victorious, and Sheldon had to look away. He swallowed, wondering if he could go now. Even though he hadn't fixed the problem, he was going to pay for it. What more could his parents want?

He headed back to the living room to grab his things. His mother was there, watching TV, and she barely looked up when he walked into the room. His father was right behind him, and he sank into his armchair, obviously satisfied.

Sheldon tightened his hands into fists. Seeing his parents like this made him angry. They weren't worried about Sheldon, or even Blake. They were only worried about themselves, and he wanted to yell at them. Instead, when he opened his mouth, he asked, "Have you heard from Blake lately?"

The room froze for a second. Then Sheldon's father glared at him. "Why would we have heard about Blake?"

"Who's Blake?" Sheldon's mother asked.

He scowled at her. "You can act as if you don't know him all you want, but he's still your son, and I'm worried about him."

"I already told you not to talk about him in this house," Sheldon's father snapped. "He's dead to us. He never existed. I don't want to hear his name, and I don't care what happened to him."

Sheldon swallowed. He wanted to push, but he already regretted asking. He'd known they wouldn't react well, so he wasn't surprised. Still, hearing his mother asking who Blake was when she'd given birth to him was a hit to the stomach. "I'm sorry," he said.

His father stared at him for a moment. Then, he nodded. "Good. You're sure you can't fix the leak?"

Sheldon hated his life. He had a good job, something Blake had always envied him, but that was it. His family was a disaster. He knew that if his parents ever found out he liked men, they would react the same way they had with Blake and kick him out of their lives. Some days, he wondered if that wouldn't be better for him. Why did he care if his parents didn't want to see him anymore? It wasn't like they loved him. They might not have kicked him out of the family the way they had Blake, but they didn't care. They'd only kept Sheldon around because he could fix things that broke in their lives, but that was it.

Sheldon missed his brother. Blake was five years younger than Sheldon, and Sheldon should have protected him. He'd tried, but he'd been frightened of losing his parents, and now, he wondered why.

"I can't fix the leak, but I told you I would pay for the plumber," he said through gritted teeth.

"Leave the money on the table by the door."

"I don't have that much money on me. I'll have to come back."

His father stared for a moment, looking like he was trying to read Sheldon's thoughts. "As long as you do."

"I already said I would."

"Good. We only cooked for two, so you should leave before dinner."

Sheldon hadn't wanted to eat with his parents, but his father's words reminded him once again how little his parents cared about him. "Of course. I'll see you soon."

His father nodded and turned his attention to the TV. When Sheldon looked at his mother, she didn't seem to notice.

Sheldon sighed and shook his head. He didn't want to be here, but he did want his parents to care about him and his brother. Instead, they could barely stand to have a conversation with him. He would be better off without them, and he couldn't wait to get out of the house.

He felt better as soon as the door closed behind him. He took a deep breath, feeling the damp air against his skin. It was going to rain, and he hoped he would be able to get back to his apartment before it did. He didn't like driving in the rain.

Blake loved the rain, though. He always had, and once again, Sheldon wondered what had happened to his brother. Even though they hadn't been as close as when they were children, they still cared for each other. Sheldon knew that Blake wouldn't have disappeared like that if he had a choice. He would have let Sheldon know what had happened to him, but he hadn't.

Sheldon swallowed. His mouth was suddenly dry at the thought that his brother wasn't answering his phone because he couldn't. Sheldon hadn't wanted Blake to work at the bar, and now, he couldn't help but wonder if maybe that was the cause of Blake's problems. Had something happened to him? Had someone hurt him? Sheldon wanted to find out, but he didn't know how. He wasn't sure that if he went to the police, they would help. Blake was an adult, and he'd been estranged from the family for a while. They would probably think he'd left.

Still, Sheldon was going to have to try. No one would help him find his brother, so he would have to do it himself. Hopefully, the police would at least attempt to find Blake, but if they didn't, well, Sheldon would have to find another way.

The door opened behind him, and he turned to see his father there, glaring. "What are you still doing here?"

"I'm going. I was just checking to see if it was raining."

"What, you're afraid of getting your hair wet?"

Sheldon almost reached for his hair, but he managed to stop before he could. He knew that even that small gesture would make his father angry. Sheldon was a man, and he shouldn't have to worry about his hair, his clothes, or any of those things, or at least, that was what Sheldon's father thought. "Of course not. I was just checking."

"Good." His father slammed the door.

Sheldon sucked in a breath. Why was he living this life again? He liked his job, but he was pretty sure he could find another one easily, possibly in another city. Then he wouldn't have to see his parents ever again.

He wouldn't see Blake either, though.

He had to find Blake. He didn't care what he would find. He had to know what had happened to his brother. Hopefully, Blake was perfectly fine and had just had an accident with his phone. That was the only reason Sheldon could think of for Blake's phone to be off. He had to cling to that thought.

He couldn't lose Blake. They only had each other, and without Blake, Sheldon was alone. More than that, though, he wanted Blake to be okay. If he'd left for whatever reason, Sheldon would be okay with it as long as he was happy.

Something at the back of Sheldon's mind told him that it couldn't be that easy. There was no way Blake would have left willingly without telling Sheldon about it, and the knowledge made Sheldon's stomach churn.

"I don't think it's wise," Morven said. He was doing his best not to glare at Orran, but he knew he was failing.

Orran crossed his arms over his chest. "The queen okayed

it."

"It doesn't mean it's wise."

"What would you have him do?"

"He left his family behind. It should be a clean break."

Blake cleared his throat. "I understand what you're saying, but I can't let my brother think I'm dead. The queen said I could call him, and I will. It's just to reassure him that I'm okay and to tell him that he won't see me again."

Morven understood why Blake wanted to do that, but he thought it was a stupid idea. He'd known what he was doing when he'd agreed to leave the human world behind and stay with the dragons. He'd chosen this, and he had to go along with it. Instead, here he was, about to call his brother and tell him he was fine. "Will you explain about dragons?" he asked.

Blake shook his head. "I promised I wouldn't. I'm not an idiot."

"I never said you were. But this is your brother we're talking about. It's one of the people you're closest to, isn't he?"

Blake's gaze flickered to Orran, and Morven almost rolled his eyes. "He is. He's the person I was the closest to until I met Orran. That's why I owe it to him to explain what happened."

"You're going to give him hope. Wouldn't it be better for him to think you're dead?"

"I can't let that happen. Sheldon was there for me when I needed him, and I know that right now, he's frantic. He's going to do something stupid to try to find me, and I can't let that happen. I promise I won't tell him where I am or about you guys. I just want him to know I'm fine."

Morven sighed. "It's not like I can forbid you to do it anyway."

"I know. I just don't want you to hate me."

Morven blinked. "Why would I hate you?"

Blake stared at him. "You're serious right now? Why *wouldn't* you hate me? I know you're Orran's best friend, and

13

you were the one closest to him until I arrived. I know you don't trust me because I'm human."

"That's not true. I never said I didn't trust you."

"But you're not trusting him with this," Orran pointed out.

Sometimes Morven wanted to strangle his best friend. "It's not that I don't trust you," he repeated, looking at Blake. "It's that it's dangerous. I know the queen told you that you could do this, but her family is still trying to knock her off the throne. They're not the only ones, either. Several of the clans have learned about your presence here, and they're using it as proof that the queen is weak. If she can't even keep a human out of the clan, who's to say that she's a good clan leader and that we can withstand attacks?"

Blake bit his lower lip. "I don't want to put the clan in danger, and I know that just my presence here does. I need to talk to Sheldon, though."

Morven could tell he wouldn't change Blake's mind. "Then call him. Explain what happened. As long as you remember that you can't tell him much, I won't say anything."

"You've already said plenty."

"Nothing I said made you change your mind. Besides, the queen agreed to this. Her orders take precedence over mine."

Blake grinned and looked down at his phone. It had been turned off since he and Orran had been on the run, and it was obvious he couldn't wait to turn it on again. Morven might think this was a bad idea, but he could understand where Blake was coming from.

He didn't know what he would do if he couldn't tell Orran or any of his other friends that he was okay. He could only imagine how Orran would feel if he thought he was dead. He would try to find him, no matter the consequences, and from what Blake was saying, the same went for his brother. Of course, Blake's brother was human, so there probably wasn't much he could do to find him, but he could put himself in danger. Blake would never forgive himself if something happened to his brother because of this, and Morven suspected that neither would Orran.

Blake lifted the phone to his ear and waited. Morven held his breath, even though he didn't much care about the outcome of this. He only cared that Blake was putting them in danger. Hopefully, he was as trustworthy as the queen and Orran thought he was—and his brother would be, too.

"Blake?" a voice asked.

Morven glared at the phone. His brother had yelled so loudly that even Morven had heard it, and he wasn't anywhere close to Blake.

"Yeah, it's me," Blake answered.

Morven didn't hear what Blake's brother answered, but he could imagine. He should probably listen in to the conversation. Even though he couldn't believe he felt like this, he *did* trust Blake not to say anything that pertained to the dragons or the palace. Instead, he turned his attention to Orran.

Orran wasn't head of security anymore. He was a tutor, and as such, he wasn't privy to the information Morven had. He'd been head of security for years, though, while Morven had only just begun. He could do with some help, or at the very least, advice.

The queen had been threatened, which was nothing new. Still, it made Morven nervous. He knew many dragons were going to try to use the fact that Blake was staying with them and was the queen's son's tutor against her. If they could topple her off the throne, they would. If that happened, they would probably kill Blake and anyone who stood in their path to him, and that included Orran.

Morven might not understand it, but he knew Orran loved Blake and nothing would change that. That meant that if Blake was threatened, Orran would step in, and Morven didn't want that to happen. He didn't want to lose his best friend, and even more importantly, he didn't want anything to happen to the queen.

She was a good leader. Her father had been before her, and a lot of elders hadn't liked the fact that she was a female. Her father hadn't seen anything wrong with that, and he'd taught her how to be a good leader. When he died, she took his place, even though some elders had tried to convince her otherwise. They'd thought she would make a good queen, but only at the side of a king.

The queen had told them to take a hike.

That was where the displeasure and hate against her were rooted, and Morven knew some people would take advantage of the fact that Blake was there.

"Thank you," Orran murmured.

When Morven looked at him, he was staring at Blake, who was still on the phone. "What are you thanking me for?"

"For allowing him to do this. I know the queen told him he could, but I'm sure that if you told her it was too dangerous, she would forbid it."

"I don't hate Blake, and I don't want him to stay away from his family. It's a necessity, though."

Orran turned his gaze toward Morven. "How are things going?"

It made Morven smile. "You're not head of security anymore, remember?"

"How could I not? You don't miss a chance to remind me. The fact that I'm not head of security anymore doesn't mean I can't advise you, though. I also want to know what's going on. I have to protect Blake."

Morven sighed. "Nothing new. The queen has been threatened, and people aren't happy about Blake's presence here. It's mostly the elders, but you know someone is going to take advantage of this sooner or later."

"I'm aware." He looked at Blake again. "I can't give him

up, though."

"I know. I'm not asking you to." Because Morven knew that if he did, he'd lose. If Blake had to leave, he had no doubt that Orran would go with him. He might not understand it, but it was clear as day, and he wasn't going to risk it. His friendship with Orran was important to him, and just as Orran would do everything he could to keep Blake safe, Morven would do the same for Orran.

Sheldon didn't know what to think. He wasn't even sure he *could* think, not with Blake on the other side of the phone. "Where are you? I'll pick you up."

Blake chuckled. "Still trying to mother me, I see."

"I'm not mothering you. I'm offering you a ride. That's it."

"We both know that's not true, but fine. I'll play along." He sighed so heavily that Sheldon could hear him for the phone. "And you can't pick me up."

"Why not? What happened to you? I've been trying to call you for days, and you never answered." It was closer to weeks, but Sheldon didn't want Blake to think he truly was overbearing. He probably was, but who could blame him? He and Blake only had each other.

"I met someone."

Sheldon blinked. That was *not* what he thought he'd hear. "You disappeared for weeks because you met a guy?"

Blake huffed. "Okay, said like that, it sounds bad. Hear me out, though."

"I'm listening, but you better give me a good reason for me not to find you wherever you are and kick your ass."

"Like I said, I met someone. A guy. He's incredible. I can't believe I was that lucky, and I'm with him right now."

"Okay. So you don't want me to pick you up. I still want to see you."

"It's not going to be possible. I'm not in the city anymore."

Sheldon had to swallow twice before he was able to speak again. "You left the city without telling me?"

"I'm sorry. I didn't mean for anything like this to happen, but I didn't have the time to warn you."

"So you're with him now?"

"I am. And I can never come back, Sheldon."

Sheldon couldn't think. He heard the words, but they didn't make sense. "What does that even mean?"

"I can't explain. The only thing I can tell you is that I'm safe and happy. I'm in love, and I hope that now that you know I'm fine, you'll be able to go on with your life. I know you were worried about me. You don't have to be, though."

"Is he forcing you?"

"What are you talking about?"

"You just said that you met someone and that you can never come back. Is he keeping you prisoner?" It was that, or Blake was lying to Sheldon, and Sheldon didn't want that to be the case.

He wanted his brother to trust him the way he'd always trusted Blake. They might have grown distant in the past few years, but it was only because of the circumstances they were in, not because Sheldon didn't love his brother anymore or because he didn't trust him.

"I'm not a prisoner. I promise you I'm safe and happy. Please, Sheldon. I can't explain."

Sheldon was already thinking about who this mystery guy could be. As far as he knew, Blake didn't have friends. He didn't go out much except for work, which meant that whoever this guy was, Blake had probably met him at the bar where he'd been working. "You won't tell me anything else?" he asked because he had to try.

"I told you what I could. Just be happy for me. I'm sorry I had to leave you behind, and if I could change things, I would.

I can't, though. That means that we can't see each other again, but we can talk on the phone."

"I suppose that's better than nothing."

Sheldon could almost hear the wincing in Blake's voice. "I know you're angry."

"You're damn right I'm angry. You disappear for weeks without telling anyone what happened to you, and when you finally call me, it's only to tell me that you met someone and that we can never see each other again. It doesn't make sense. Are you in a cult? Are you lying?"

"I'm not."

"You're not telling me everything, though. That's a lie by omission."

"I'm telling you what I can. Please, Sheldon. This is important to me. I need you to stay away. You can't try to find me. You wouldn't be able to anyway, and I don't want you to get in trouble. I called you because I wanted you to know I was fine."

"You're not fine. If you can't tell me what's going on, I'll *have* to find out on my own."

"You're infuriating. You can't find out on your own. You're going to get hurt, and it'll be your fault because you wouldn't listen to me. Can't you do that for once?"

"You left me!" Sheldon sucked in a breath. He hadn't meant to burst out the way he had, but it wasn't a lie.

Blake was silent for a moment, and Sheldon wondered if he'd hung up. He tightened his hold on the phone and waited.

"I'm sorry," Blake finally said. "I never wanted to leave you. You know what my life was like, though. You have your job and a family, but I had nothing."

"My job is boring, and our family would hate me if they knew."

"What are you talking about?"

Sheldon shook his head even though Blake couldn't see

him. "Never mind that. They kicked you out. They act as if you never existed. I don't care if I have them. I don't want them. I want *you*."

"I'm touched, but it's better this way. Now, you know I'm happy. I have my own life. I have a job and a man I love."

"And you're leaving me behind for that."

"I wouldn't if I didn't have to. You have to believe that."

"How can I believe it when I have no idea what's happening?"

"This is all I can tell you. I'm sorry, Sheldon. I hope you'll understand eventually."

Sheldon knew what Blake was doing. "Don't you dare hang up on me. You have no right to. I want answers, and you're going to give them to me."

But Sheldon could already hear the beeping that told him that Blake had hung up.

He lowered his phone and stared at it. Then, he blindly sat on the couch.

He was glad his brother was okay, but he was also worried. Something was happening for Blake to tell him that he couldn't see him ever again. Sheldon didn't know what it was, but he *would* find out. He wasn't abandoning Blake. Their family already had, but Sheldon was different. His brother needed him. Even if he wasn't lying, he wasn't telling Sheldon everything, which meant something was going on. Blake might still be in danger, and Sheldon had to do something about it.

What, though? He wasn't going just to accept the fact that they couldn't see each other again without fighting. Blake should have known that, and maybe he had. He wasn't wrong when he said that Sheldon had no way to find him, though. Sheldon didn't even know where to start.

He'd gone to Blake's apartment, but Blake hadn't been there. The place had been abandoned, and Sheldon had had to pack his brother's things and put them away when the landlord had realized Blake wouldn't be back. The boxes were still in his living room, where he could see them every day.

The only other place he knew where to look was the bar where Blake had worked. Sheldon didn't want to go there, but he knew he was going to have to. No matter how little he liked it, it was his only link to his brother, and he wouldn't waste it. He was going to find Blake whether Blake liked it or not.

Chapter Two

Sheldon stared at the bar in front of him. He didn't want to go in. The only thing he wanted to do was turn around and run home. This wasn't his kind of place, and he had a hard time imagining Blake working here.

It was seedy, to say the least. Sheldon wouldn't be here if it weren't for Blake, and even then, he'd almost gone home as soon as he'd arrived. He had to find his brother, though. Since Blake hadn't told him the truth about what had happened to him and why he wasn't coming back, Sheldon was going to have to find him on his own.

He hoped he wouldn't regret it.

He swallowed, clutched his car keys, and moved forward.

As soon as he stepped inside, the smell of beer, sweat, and cloying perfume hit him in the face. He sucked in a breath and immediately regretted it. He grimaced, but he didn't back down. Now that he was here, he couldn't. Instead, he walked deeper into the bar and looked around.

To the right, high stools butted up against a high counter. Several men were sitting there, and behind it, a bartender was freshening drinks and filling orders. Sheldon had to swallow again at the thought that his brother had once done this. Blake wouldn't have looked out of place here, but he certainly did, and he could feel people looking at him.

He straightened his back and raised his chin high. Then he strode toward the bar.

He sat on one of the stools, snatching his hand away from the counter when he felt it was sticky. He rubbed his fingertips on his thighs, and when the bartender came toward him, ordered a beer. He wanted water, but he didn't want to look even more out of place than he already was.

The clink of glass against the counter made him jerk, but he nodded at the bartender and took the beer. "Can I ask you a question?" he asked.

The bartender frowned. "Depends. What do you want to know?"

"The guy who worked here before you. You know what happened to him?"

The bartender shook his head. "No idea."

"Do you know if there's anyone here I could ask? Maybe your boss?"

The bartender stared at Sheldon for a bit. Sheldon took a sip of beer, hoping to look more comfortable, but the beer was bitter, and he didn't like bitter. He should have known better than to order it.

"Trust me, you don't want to talk to the boss," the bartender finally said.

"I *have* to talk to him. My brother used to work here, and he vanished. I have to find him."

"Talking to the boss isn't going to help you with that."

"But he's the only person I can talk to."

The bartender shrugged one shoulder. "Your loss. I tried to warn you." He tilted his chin toward the end of the counter. "That's Hans. He's the boss, and he might know something about your brother."

Sheldon paid for the beer but was more than happy to leave it on the counter. He slid off the stool and headed toward Hans, hoping his footsteps were steadier than he felt. He rubbed his palms on his sides, then stopped in front of Hans.

It took Hans a moment to realize Sheldon was there. When he did, he arched a brow. "What do you want?"

"To talk about my brother."

"Who's your brother?"

"His name is Blake. He used to work here, but he disappeared several weeks ago, and I haven't heard from him since."

Something glinted in Hans's gaze. "You're Blake's brother?"

"I am. Do you know what happened to him?"

"I might. Why don't you follow me to my office?"

Sheldon's heart raced. He didn't want to go anywhere with Hans, but this was the only way for him to find his brother. "Sure. Lead the way."

Sheldon could have sworn people were staring at him as he followed Hans away from the bar. He kept his gaze forward, not wanting to see it. He didn't care why they stared. He just wanted to know that Blake truly was okay.

Hans led him down a hallway. He entered a room at the end of it, and Sheldon expected an office, just like Hans had said. Instead, it was a mostly bare room. The floors were cement, and while there was a table with several chairs in the middle, that was it. Two men were sitting around the table, but they looked up when they heard the door.

"This guy here is Blake's brother," Hans said.

The two men got to their feet. Sheldon took a step back. "I think I'm just going to leave," he said.

Hans grinned at him. "Not until I have answers. Sit down. We have to talk."

Sheldon's hands were shaking, but he knew he had to obey. Blake had warned him not to get himself into trouble, yet that was what he'd done.

He shouldn't have come. He regretted it, mostly because he could tell that he wouldn't find anything about Blake. It had been a mistake, because Hans clearly didn't know what had happened to Sheldon's brother.

"Have you heard from him at all?" Hans asked.

"Yes, but—"

Hans reached for Sheldon's pocket. Sheldon jerked away, but one of the men pushed on his shoulders, forcing him to sit down again. Hans wiggled his hand into Sheldon's pocket and took out his cell phone. He held it out and stared at Sheldon until Sheldon unlocked it, then grinned again. He thumbed through the phone, and when he stopped, Sheldon knew who he was going to call.

"He's not going to answer," he warned

To his surprise, Hans handed him the phone. "No? Well, you better hope he does. Talk to your brother. Tell him I'm looking for him and that he has to pay me back for the egg."

Sheldon blinked. "The egg?"

Hans leaned closer. His breath smelled of beer, and it made Sheldon want to jerk back. He couldn't move, though, not with one of the goons still holding him by the shoulders.

"He stole a dragon egg from me. I don't take being robbed nicely, and especially not a dragon egg. Do you know how much profit I could have gotten from it?"

Sheldon didn't know in detail, but he could imagine. What had Blake got himself into? He hadn't mentioned any of this to Sheldon. Instead, he talked about a guy he'd met. Who was that guy? Did he have anything to do with this stolen egg?

"Call him," Hans said. His tone was threatening now, and Sheldon knew something bad would happen to him if he didn't obey.

Sheldon nodded and looked at his phone. He hoped Blake would answer. It had taken him weeks to call Sheldon, but hopefully, now that he had, he would be reachable. If he wasn't, Sheldon didn't know what would happen to him, but unfortunately for him, he could too easily imagine.

Morven's arms were crossed over his chest. He stared at the scene in front of him, and he was working hard not to smile.

Today he was standing guard with Blue, Blake, and Orran. It wasn't part of his usual job, but he'd wanted to get away from his office for a bit, and this was the perfect solution. It allowed him to spend time with his best friend and to make sure Blue was okay.

That was what everyone was afraid of. Some dragons were trying to topple the queen off her throne, and they might try to do it through her son. After all, Blue would one day take her place. And if people could make sure that didn't happen, they wouldn't stop for anything. Morven wouldn't put it past any of them to hurt the little dragon, and he wouldn't allow that to happen.

"How long is it going to take him to shift into a human?" Blake asked. Blue was climbing his shoulders, but he didn't seem to care. The baby dragon made a triumphant noise when he got to Blake's shoulder, and Blake reached to the side without even looking at him, gently stroking his forehead.

Morven was pretty sure that a lot of people would have been offended at the casual way Blake behaved with Blue. Blue wasn't just a baby dragon. He was the heir to the throne, and he ought to be treated that way. Blake didn't seem to care, though. He treated Blue as if he were just a normal baby, and it made Morven like him more.

Morven didn't understand the needs and duties of being a queen, but he could imagine they would be much too heavy for the little dragon's shoulders. For now, he got to be just a baby, and it was good. It was going to take years for him to be ready to take his mother's place anyway. He had more than enough time to learn everything there was to know about being a king, but for now, he was playing around and having fun.

"There's no way to know," Orran said. He was smiling,

too, although Morven wondered if it was because of Blue or because of Blake.

"When do you guys usually first shift into human form?"

"Once we start walking."

"He's already walking."

"As a human, I mean. It's not a rule, but it makes it easier, because we don't feel confined in either form. Right now, if he were to shift into a human, he would be stuck. He's only a few weeks old."

"But human babies can take more than a year to start walking. I want to meet him in his human form." There was a pout in Blake's voice, and Morven almost snorted.

Orran didn't, though. Instead, he leaned forward and rubbed Blue's chin. "You have to learn patience. Yes, it's going to take a while, but you have all the time in the world here with us."

Morven looked away when Orran and Blake kissed. It wasn't anything wild—they wouldn't do that in front of Blue—but it still made Morven feel like he was intruding.

He startled when a phone started ringing. He looked around, wondering who had it, only mildly surprised to see Blake looked sheepish. Morven narrowed his eyes at him. "Why do you have your phone on you? And why is it on?"

"I just wanted to make sure I could talk to my brother if he tried calling me."

"You're having a lesson with Blue."

"He has to go to bed anyway. You know Sheldon didn't take this well. I wanted to make sure he wouldn't do anything stupid."

Morven rolled his eyes, but he didn't add anything. He understood where Blake was coming from, even though he didn't like it.

He turned around and gestured at one of the nannies who took care of the baby. "Take him to his rooms and bathe him.

We'll see him tomorrow."

The dragon nodded and waited for Blake to put Blue on her back. Blue cried out, but he knew better than to try to convince Blake to keep him with him. He'd tried sneaking into Blake and Orran's rooms in the beginning, but his mother had been clear with him. He would see Blake and Orran during his lessons, and he could play with them, but they weren't his parents. She was, and he had to obey her rules. He probably hadn't understood everything she'd told him, but even though he clearly wanted to stay with Blake and Orran, he went with his nanny.

As soon as he was out the door, Blake took his phone out. It had stopped ringing, then had started again, and Blake smiled when he saw the name on the screen. "It's Sheldon." He raised the phone and answered. "I thought I told you that we shouldn't talk again," he said.

Morven couldn't hear the other side of the conversation, but he could tell something was wrong from Blake's expression. His eyes widened, and he paled so much that Orran stepped closer to him and pressed a hand against his back.

"What are you doing there? Didn't you hear me tell you that you shouldn't get in trouble?" he asked.

Orran leaned closer and murmured something, and Blake nodded. He lowered his phone, hit a button on the screen, and a voice filled the room.

"I'm sorry. I had to find you and make sure you really were okay," a man said. It had to be Sheldon.

Morven liked his voice. It was smooth, even though it shook slightly, probably with fear. Morven had heard fear enough times to recognize it.

"What does he want?" Blake asked.

There was a pause, and Sheldon talked to someone who wasn't on the phone. "An egg. Either that or a baby dragon. It's the only way he'll let me go."

"I can't give him an egg or a baby."

"He's going to hurt me if you don't."

Blake looked at Morven and Orran. Morven shook his head, already knowing they couldn't help Blake's brother. To his surprise, Orran nodded. "Tell him we'll find an egg," he said.

Morven stepped closer to his best friend, not sure what to do. Why had he promised that? They couldn't hand over an egg to anyone, and especially not to someone who had already stolen one and had been planning on selling it.

They were lucky that Blake had stepped in and saved the egg. If he hadn't, Blue would have been in trouble. As it was, Blake and Orran had had to trek through the forest with Blue to reach the palace. It was during that time they'd fallen in love.

None of that mattered right now, though.

Blake looked like he couldn't quite believe Orran's words, but he still told his brother, "You heard that? We'll get you an egg. Where are you?"

"At the bar for now."

There was a noise, and then the next voice didn't belong to Sheldon. "Hello, Blake."

Blake looked like he wanted to reach through the phone and strangle whoever was talking. "Hans. Why did you take my brother?"

"Because I can get a dragon through him. We won't be at the bar when you arrive. I'll text you the directions. You only have a few days until I kill your brother. You better hurry."

He hung up, and even though Blake tried to call back, no one answered. His eyes were wide when he looked up. "We have to help him."

"We can't give this man an egg or a baby," Morven said. "I won't allow either of you to do that."

Orran glared at him. "You really think I would?"

"It's what you said."

"Because we needed to know where Sheldon is. It's the only way we have to get to him and rescue him."

Morven blinked. He should have realized that, but he hadn't even thought about saving Blake's brother. He supposed that in his mind, Sheldon was a human, and therefore, he wasn't their business. It looked like it was going to be, though. "We have to talk to the queen first."

Orran nodded. "I know. Let's go."

They couldn't be sure she would allow them to go, but for Blake's sake, Morven hoped she would. He'd saved her son, even though he hadn't known anything about where Blue came from or who he was. Even though Morven didn't understand him and was wary, Blake wasn't a bad man. He'd sacrificed his entire life to help Blue, and maybe, this was one way for them to repay him.

Sheldon had no idea what was happening. He understood the words Hans was saying, but they didn't make sense. What had Blake done? What was that about a dragon egg? And where was Blake supposed to find one to exchange for Sheldon?

Instead of giving the phone back to Sheldon, Hans put it on the table. He looked satisfied, and Sheldon knew it wouldn't be good for him or anyone else involved. "See? It wasn't that hard."

"I have no idea what you're talking about. What's going on?"

"I see your brother hasn't told you what he did." Hans tsked. "You see, I gave him a job. I was generous. And to thank me, he stole something precious from me."

"A dragon egg." It made sense. Blake wasn't stupid, and he would have known the kind of man his boss was. Hans was ready to take Sheldon hostage and use him as leverage to get what he wanted. He wasn't a good person.

"Exactly. He stuck his nose in my closet and stole my egg. Now, I have something that belongs to him. If he wants you back, he'll give me what I want."

"Where is he supposed to find a dragon egg?" Sheldon cried out.

"I don't care. He can bring me back the dragon if the egg hatched. But if he doesn't, well, let's just say you won't like what happens to you."

Sheldon didn't have to ask to know what Hans was talking about. If Blake didn't bring him a dragon or an egg, Sheldon would probably end up dead somewhere.

Blake was going to have to choose, and Sheldon wasn't sure he could. He knew his brother. Blake would want to help him, but he wouldn't want to sacrifice anyone for it, let alone a baby. Even though dragons were animals, Blake had a soft spot for them, and Sheldon didn't know what he would do. There was no way he could find a dragon or an egg. Maybe he still had the one he'd stolen, but Sheldon doubted it. Besides, Blake had said he was with people he trusted. Maybe they had something to do with the egg. Either way, he wouldn't be the one making all the decisions, and Sheldon was afraid.

What if the people Blake was staying with didn't want him to help Sheldon? What if they weren't ready to give up a dragon egg? He didn't want to die or be hurt. But if he was honest, he also didn't want a baby *anything* to get hurt.

Hans leaned closer, and Sheldon moved back. There was nowhere for him to go, not unless he got up from the chair, and he doubted he would be allowed. "You see, everything will work well. Your brother gets you back, and I get my dragon back."

"He won't bring you the egg."

"Well, I hope for your sake that he will." He straightened and looked at the two men in the room with them. "Tie him to the chair. We'll take him away later tonight."

He left the room, and Sheldon was left with the two goons. He wasn't surprised when they moved to tie him up right away. He didn't even try to fight, because he knew it wouldn't change anything even if he did. He was weak, and he couldn't fight against two men.

Once he was tied to the chair, they left, too. Unfortunately, it gave Sheldon too much time to think about all his mistakes.

He shouldn't have come. He should have trusted his brother. Blake had told him he was safe and that he was happy, and instead of believing him, Sheldon had needed to see it with his own two eyes. Now, he was in the hands of people who would think nothing of hurting him to get what they wanted. He was forcing Blake's hand, and he didn't know how the situation would go. Even if Blake could get a dragon egg, he wouldn't want to hand it over to Hans. Sheldon didn't want him to, either, but if he had to choose between himself and the egg, he already knew what he would do.

There was no good way out of this. Sheldon wasn't sure there was *any* way out of this, period.

He swallowed and looked around. The room was empty, and he doubted he could find anything that would work as a weapon or untie his hands. The bar wasn't empty, though. There was music, but people were bound to hear him if he screamed, right?

There was only one way for him to find out. He swallowed, then licked his lips because his mouth was dry. He was terrified, but he hated feeling helpless, even though he knew he was. Hans wouldn't be happy if Sheldon started screaming, but if Sheldon had only one chance to make it out, he had to try.

He opened his mouth and screamed for help.

The queen had already retired in her rooms for the night, but there was a way to contact her. Morven shifted as soon as they were out of the classroom.

Your Majesty?

It took a moment for her to answer. *Morven? What is it?*

Orran and I need to talk to you. It's about Blake's brother.

Blake's brother? What's going on?

We'll explain everything once we're with you. Is it all right if we come?

I suppose it is. Give me a moment to put Blue to bed, and I'll be right with you. Wait in my living room.

Morven shifted back to tell Orran and Blake what the queen had said. He wished he could stay in his dragon form, but he was getting used to being in his human one, and he wanted Blake to understand him. "She'll listen to what we have to say."

"Have you told her about my brother?" Blake asked.

"I haven't told her what happened, just that he was involved. We can explain once we're with her. Come on. She told me to wait in her living room."

At this moment, Morven was glad he was head of security. It meant he didn't have to answer to anyone and that the guards didn't try to stop him when he strode toward the queen's quarters. It wasn't the first time Morven had to wait in the living room, and he knew exactly where to go.

He couldn't help but wonder how strange the palace must be to Blake. Everything was made for dragons in their dragon form, and he looked kind of tiny in it. He didn't seem to care at the moment. There was no doubt he was focused on his brother and what was happening to him, and Morven didn't blame him. From what he'd heard, whoever had Sheldon wouldn't be nice to him. They wanted a dragon egg, and they were ready to do anything to get it.

When the queen arrived, she was in her human form, too. Morven wasn't surprised. She knew Blake was involved, and she wouldn't be able to talk to him if she stayed in her dragon form.

"What's going on?" she asked.

"I'm sorry to bother you, your Majesty," Blake started. "I just got a phone call from my brother. He was captured by the men who took Blue from you."

The queen frowned. "Explain."

"I don't have much to say. I got a phone call, and it was my brother. The man who took him wants either a dragon egg or a baby dragon, and if I give him that, he'll give me back my brother. Otherwise . . ." Blake didn't have to explain for everyone in the room to know what would happen to Sheldon if he didn't obey.

"I told the man we would obey," Orran said. "He already sent the coordinates to the place in which we're supposed to take the egg."

"You're planning on rescuing Blake's brother," the queen said.

"I am. I know we never talked about having two humans here, but for a few days, I don't think it will be a problem."

Morven sucked in a breath. It was a risk to ask this from the queen. She could say no, both to letting Sheldon stay with them and to rescuing him. Morven suspected that if that was the case, Blake could go on his own, which meant that Orran would want to go with him. If that happened, Morven would go, too. He didn't want to disobey orders, but he would quit his job if he had to. It was important to him, as was the clan, but Orran was more important. He was Morven's best friend, and Morven was ready to do anything to help him.

"What do you have in mind?" the queen asked.

"We'll go to the address the man sent us. We won't be

taking an egg or a baby with us, though. It would be better if we were several people strong, but even if only I go, it shouldn't be a problem. I'll help Sheldon and bring him here, if you agree, of course. He can lay low for a few days, and once we're sure everything is over, he can either go home or somewhere else."

The queen slowly nodded. "You're planning on going alone?"

"He's not going alone," Blake snapped. He seemed to realize how harsh he'd been and cleared his throat. "I apologize. But I won't allow Orran to go on his own. Sheldon is my brother, and I want to help him."

"You're human. You'll get hurt," Orran said.

"You could get hurt, too. It's not going to stop you, is it?"

"It's not, but it doesn't mean you should come. I can shift into a dragon. You can't."

"Maybe not, but I know Hans. He was my boss, remember? I know exactly how he thinks and what he's planning on doing. I'm pretty sure he expects us to try to save Sheldon and not give him anything. He's not stupid. You're going to need me. Even if you didn't, though, I would still want to go with you."

"As do I," Morven said.

The queen turned her attention to him. "You do realize I can't agree to this."

"With all due respect, your Majesty, if I can't go, I'll resign from my post as head of security."

Someone sucked in a breath, either Orran or Blake, but Morven kept his attention on the queen. He didn't want to disobey orders, but he was going to do this, whether she wanted him to or not.

"You're ready to disobey a direct order for a human?" she asked.

"I'm ready to disobey a direct order for Orran. We both

know he'll do this whether or not we want him to. I don't want him to go on his own. He'll get hurt. He needs help, and he'll get it. I don't want to resign, but I'll do it if I have to."

The queen sighed. "All right. I suppose I can do without you for a few days. The two of you won't be going alone, though. Take the rest of your team. You'll need them."

Morven had a hard time believing she'd agree to this, but he wasn't going to protest. Blake opened his mouth, no doubt to tell her that he would be going, too, but Orran grabbed his hand and shook his head. Blake looked angry, but thankfully, he didn't add anything.

"Thank you, Your Majesty," Orran said.

She shook her head. "Don't thank me. I owe Blake. I always will. He saved my son, and if I can ever help him, I will. Even though I'm wary of having two humans staying with us, I understand family, and that's who Sheldon is. Go. Get Sheldon back and bring him home."

"You mean here?" Blake asked hesitantly.

The queen smiled at him. "It *is* your home, isn't it?"

"It is, but I know that my presence here is causing trouble. I don't want things to get worse with my brother here, too."

"You let me worry about that. Indeed, your presence here isn't making things easy for me, but it's not your fault."

"You wouldn't have these problems if I weren't here."

"That's where you're wrong. I would. Your presence here is only an excuse for the people who want to topple me off the throne. If you weren't here, they would find another reason."

"Still, I'm sorry for bringing so much trouble to you."

"Don't worry about it. Get your brother back. We can talk about everything else later."

They had their orders, even though they were different from what Morven had expected. He'd thought the queen would want to leave Sheldon in that man's hands, or at the very least, that she wouldn't send him since he was head of security. She no doubt understood that he was serious about resigning if she didn't allow this rescue mission to happen.

They left the queen's rooms, and once out in the hallway, they looked at each other. "I didn't think she would agree," Blake murmured.

Morven surprised even himself by clapping Blake's shoulder and squeezing. "But she did. We have work to do. I suppose that asking you to stay here isn't going to work?"

Blake shook his head. "I can't agree with staying back when you go. I know I'm nowhere near as good as the two of you at fighting, and like you pointed out, I'm not a dragon shifter. I want to be there, though. Sheldon won't understand what's happening. He's already freaking out as it is. It's going to be even worse if a bunch of dragons attacks the place where he's kept and kidnaps him. You're going to need me. Trust me."

Morven suspected he was right. "Let's go, then. We have work to do."

CHAPTER THREE

Sheldon had no idea where he was. Last night, after he'd spent a while in the room at the bar, he'd been taken away. He'd been blindfolded, stuffed into a car trunk, and moved. He'd also been beaten, which was why his entire body hurt. He was dirty, hungry, and terrified. He also didn't know what time it was, although he could see a patch of sky from a broken window, so he knew it was still dark and probably night.

He needed more. Having no idea where he was or what time it was made him feel lost, although he supposed it was one reason Hans had done it. He wanted Blake to pay for what he'd done, and he was doing it through Sheldon. Sheldon didn't doubt that if Blake came, Hans would take pleasure in hurting Sheldon even more.

Sheldon knew his brother would come. They'd always been there for each other, and this time wasn't any different. He'd heard how freaked out Blake had been on the phone, and Sheldon knew his brother would do everything he could to get him back.

What Sheldon didn't know was whether or not Blake would succeed. He knew Hans, but he was still only one man. Even if he had help from whoever he'd fallen in love with, it wasn't a guarantee that Sheldon would make it out of this in one piece. He was pretty sure at least a few bones were already broken, and even though he barely knew Hans, he had no doubt that by the time Blake got here, he would be in even worse shape.

Blake would come, but he wouldn't be able to fulfill his

side of the deal. Where would he find a dragon egg? He might still have the one he'd stolen, but Sheldon doubted it. And if the egg had hatched, Blake had no doubt released the dragon into the wild. There was no way for him to get another one, which meant he would come empty-handed. Hans would take his anger out on both Blake and Sheldon, and if they were lucky, they would be left for dead. If they weren't, well, they would probably *be* dead.

Sheldon had thought his life was boring, but right now, he wanted to get back to it desperately.

A door slammed in the distance, making him jump. He peered at the door with half-closed eyes, wondering if someone had come for him. Could Blake already be here? Maybe Sheldon had been unconscious longer than he'd thought. Maybe an entire day had passed, giving Blake time to arrive. Sheldon wouldn't be surprised. He'd been in and out of consciousness after he'd been beaten, and he was pretty sure he had a concussion.

The door to his cell creaked open, and two men came in. One of them was one of the goons from the bar, but the other one was new. It wouldn't help, but Sheldon still had to try. "Let me go, please. I promise I won't say anything."

The two men barely even looked at him. Instead, they untied him from the chair he was in. Sheldon's heart skipped a beat. They were taking him out of the cell, which meant Blake had arrived. Well, either that or they were going to beat him some more. He hoped the first one was right. He wasn't sure he could withstand a second beating.

He tried to walk, but his legs felt like jelly. One of the men who had beaten him had taken great pleasure in kicking his legs, and he couldn't help but wonder if a bone or two hadn't been broken there, too. The two men dragging him didn't seem to care. They kept on pulling, even when he stumbled and almost fell on his face. He supposed he should be grateful their hold had kept him upright. Right now, though, he didn't feel grateful for much.

He blinked when they stepped into the hallway. The cell he'd been in had been dark, but harsh white light flooded the rest of wherever he was. The men dragged him down the hallway, which ended at a metal door. One of them pushed it open, and Sheldon held his breath.

It was only a hallway, though. They continued walking, and he could feel his strength leaving him. It was a mix of not having eaten in a while and being beaten. He'd lost some blood, and that probably had something to do with how weak he was feeling, too. He hoped that whatever was about to happen happened fast. He wasn't sure he could power through anything longer than a few minutes.

When they crossed the next door, they were finally outside. It was cold, but Sheldon still took in a deep breath. He'd thought he would never see this again. He'd thought these men would kill him and bury his body somewhere, and that no one would ever know what had happened to him. They still might, but at least Sheldon had seen the sky one last time.

The relief only lasted a few seconds. Then, he looked ahead and saw Blake standing there alone.

Sheldon sucked in a breath. "You have to go," he yelled at his brother.

One of the men slapped the back of his head, but Sheldon didn't care. He was already in pain. Another slap here and there wasn't going to change anything.

Blake shook his head. "I'm here to help you."

"You can't help me, not on your own. Go." If Sheldon had to choose between himself and his brother, he would sacrifice himself without a second thought.

Blake shook his head. "Trust me. Please."

Sheldon opened his mouth to answer, but one of the men twisted and punched him in the face. The pain was harsh and strong, and Sheldon's knees buckled. This time, the two men let him go, and he crumbled to the ground.

"You saw that we have him," Hans said.

Sheldon hadn't even seen him standing there. He was at the side of the door, staring at Blake.

"I also see that you've hurt him," Blake snapped.

"What did you expect? You stole my dragon egg. You're lucky he's only a little banged up and that he's not missing any limbs."

"Let him go."

"I don't think so. You have what I asked for?"

"I do. You're going to have to let him go if you want it, though."

I don't think so. You know, I've wanted revenge on you since you stole my egg. You made me look like a fool, and I don't like that."

"So you took my brother?"

"I did, and now I have the two of you. It'll be fun to make you watch when I kill your brother."

Sheldon sucked in a breath and tried to get to his feet, but one of the goons pushed him back down. He stayed there, folded onto himself, the ground digging into his palms.

He had to do something. He needed to save his brother, but how? He barely had any strength, and he was alone.

He'd known Blake would come, but now he wished his brother hadn't. They were both going to die, and it would be Sheldon's fault. He should have listened to Blake. He shouldn't have gone looking, and now he'd ruined everything. His brother had sounded happy on the phone, and Sheldon should have believed that instead of thinking Blake was lying to him. He was going to be both of their downfalls, and he would never forgive himself for that.

He supposed that since he was going to die soon, at least the regrets wouldn't be there for long.

"You'll never find the egg if you kill me," Blake pointed out.

"I don't have to wait for you to tell me where it is. Torture goes a long way when it comes to getting answers."

"You can't," Sheldon said, but no one paid attention to him.

Blake took a step closer, reaching for Sheldon, but he stopped. He looked at Hans, and Sheldon could see how much he hated the man. "There's a problem with this plan," he said.

Hans blinked. "There is?"

Sheldon thought Blake had gone mad for a second because he grinned. It all made sense when Blake added, "You think I'm here alone, but I'm not."

Morven landed in front of Blake with the rest of his team. He was glad all of them were there. It would make it easier to grab Sheldon and go.

No matter how much Morven wanted to snatch Hans and slam him to the ground until he was dead for what he did to dragons, he couldn't. This was purely a rescue mission and nothing else. Still, the fact that they were all present meant there were five dragons to save one man. It made it easy, which meant they might have the time to make sure Hans would never hurt anyone else.

Orran had already agreed to dedicate himself to Blake's safety. No one had been surprised, and even though Blake insisted he could deal with this on his own, Morven suspected he was relieved. It couldn't be easy to see his brother in the state he was in. Morven didn't know the man, but even he was furious at the sight.

He'd imagined Sheldon would be like Blake, but he'd been wrong. He couldn't see much resemblance between them, because Sheldon's face was swollen, but even his body was different. Blake was taller and better built. Sheldon, on the other hand, was slight. His hair had once been neat, where Blake's was shaggy, and of course, he was beaten up.

The fact that they were only three men pointed to the fact that Hans had thought he could grab Blake, too. He'd screeched when he'd seen the dragons and tried to run, but Hogan grabbed him.

What do you want me to do with him? Hogan asked.

Whatever you want. I don't care.

Hogan grinned, which in his dragon form was terrifying. Hans squeaked, but when he tried to scramble away, Hogan tightened his hold on him. Morven could tell by the way Hans's face went red.

With Hans taken care of, Morven turned his attention to the two men who'd brought Sheldon out. Octavia and Slavin had each grabbed one, which left Morven with nothing to do but focus on Sheldon.

"I told you it wouldn't be dangerous," he heard Blake mumble.

When he turned to look at Blake, he was hidden behind Orran, who was refusing to allow him to go to his brother. It didn't take much, only for Orran to take a step to the side following which direction Blake was going. Morven huffed in laughter, and of course, Blake noticed it. He turned and glared at him.

"Why don't you go grab him? We need to get out of here, no matter how much fun you're having stomping people into the ground."

Morven winced when he realized that was what Octavia was doing. There wasn't much left of the goon she'd picked.

He nodded and moved forward toward Sheldon. He was still curled up on the ground, and Morven thought he was unconscious until he looked up. His eyes widened, and he tried to scramble to his feet, but Morven snatched him and took flight before Sheldon could try anything. The man was screaming and trying to get away, but there was no moving Morven.

Let's go, he told everyone.

Already? I was having fun, Octavia answered.

You can have fun at home.

It's not the same. These people were horrible.

I'm sure we can find you horrible people to stomp on back at the palace, too. We shouldn't linger. There were only three men outside, but we don't know how many there are inside. Besides, Sheldon was still screaming, and it was starting to make Morven's head ache.

Once everyone was in the air, they headed toward the edge of the city. They would have to land soon to make sure Sheldon was okay and to reassure him, but Morven wanted to put some distance between them and the city. It would be smart if they stayed out for the next day and maybe the next night, just in case someone had noticed them and was following them, but he couldn't imagine it would be great to camp out with two humans. He and the other dragon shifters usually stayed in their dragon form when they did so, which meant they weren't cold, and even if it rained, it wasn't a problem. It was also easier for them to hunt and eat in that form. They couldn't do that with two humans around, though, especially when one of those humans was Sheldon.

Who was still screaming.

Morven sighed. *Blake wasn't kidding when he said his brother was going to freak out,* he projected to his friends.

Slavin laughed, and Morven glared at him.

He warned you, Orran pointed out.

Is there anything he can do? I can't fly for much longer with a screeching man hanging from my hand. Besides, he's going to draw attention, and that's the last thing we want.

Morven could feel everyone was amused, but thankfully, they didn't add anything. Instead, Orran flew closer to him until the brothers could see each other. They were both hanging from a dragon's hand, and when Sheldon saw Blake, he snapped his mouth shut.

Finally, Morven said in relief.

Slavin laughed again.

Morven kept his focus on where he was going, but he couldn't avoid hearing what the brothers were saying to each other.

"You have to calm down," Blake explained.

"*Calm down?* A dragon just kidnapped me. How am I supposed to calm down? It's going to eat me, isn't it? We're both going to die."

"We're not. I promise you that. I have a lot of things to tell you, but I can't do it now. Calm down and relax, and as soon as we land, I'll explain everything."

"How can you take be so calm? You should be freaking out."

"I did the first time."

"The first time?" Sheldon screeched.

A rumble of laughter came from Slavin, and Sheldon snapped his attention to him. "That one is going to enjoy eating me."

"None of them are going to eat you. I promise. Things aren't the way they seem."

Will you stop looking at him like he's dinner? Morven asked Slavin.

I'm not. I just find him amusing.

Well, find him amusing in silence. We don't want to freak out the human.

You know, I thought I wouldn't like humans, but I kind of do.

Morven glared at him. *Don't let him know that, or he'll think you're going to nibble his toes or something.*

Slavin laughed. Sheldon tried to scramble out of Morven's hand.

"I'm serious," Blake said. "Calm down. You're going to

hurt Morven, and he might drop you. We're here to help you, not to hurt you."

"You named your dragons?" Sheldon sounded incredulous.

As if I'd allow Blake to name me, Morven grumbled.

You'd allow the love of my life to do anything he wants if it made me happy, Orran pointed out.

He was probably right.

"They're not my dragons." Blake sounded amused.

"Whose dragons are they, then?"

"It's a long story, but I promise I'll explain as soon as we land. Trust me. I know you don't have a reason to after the way I behaved with you, but I promise you're not going to get hurt, not any more than you already are. They're here to help you, not to hurt you."

"I want to know right now."

Morven sighed. They should have known Sheldon wouldn't take this well. They *had* known it, but none of them had expected for him to scream his head off.

"I don't think I can tell you, not now," Blake said. He had to yell for his brother to hear him.

Let him know he can, Morven told Orran. He wasn't sure how Orran would relay the message, but if it made Sheldon stop screaming, he was all for it.

He didn't think it would matter when Blake told his brother that they were shifters. Sheldon would find out sooner or later, and he might as well do so here, where he couldn't run away.

Sheldon was flying. Well, he wasn't actually doing the flying, but he was in the air, and if he looked down, he would freak out. He'd never realized how afraid he was of heights until now, but now that he did, he swore he was never going to fly again.

Not that he would have the occasion. He was probably going to die tonight, either eaten by a dragon or splattered on the ground.

Instead of answering, Blake looked up at the dragon carrying him. The dragon looked down, and Sheldon could have sworn he smiled. That didn't make sense, and he held his breath.

None of this made sense. Where had Blake been? Why was he hanging around with five dragons? Where were the dragons taking them? Blake seemed to have a lot of the answers Sheldon was seeking, and Sheldon wanted all of them. He knew he couldn't demand anything, but he hoped his brother would answer. He needed to know what was happening. It was the only way for him to stop freaking out, and Blake knew it as well as Sheldon.

Blake turned his attention back to Sheldon. "All right. I'll tell you."

Sheldon narrowed his eyes. "Did the dragon tell you that you could?"

"In a way."

"They're animals."

Blake grinned. "That's where you're wrong. They're *not* animals. They're people, just like us."

"Have you hit your head? Is that why you're hanging around with dragons? Do you have a concussion?"

Blake huffed and shook his head. "I knew you wouldn't believe me without seeing proof. You'll get it as soon as we land. But I can promise you we're safe, so please, stop screaming. I'm pretty sure Morven is going to eat you if you don't."

Sheldon looked up. The dragon who was carrying him was impressive. He'd known dragons looked different from each other, but he'd never seen one in the flesh. All his knowledge on them came from books and movies, and he was pretty sure there'd been mistakes.

The dragon above him was green. The color went from light to dark, and it was beautiful. It was dark, so Sheldon couldn't see as much of the dragon as he wanted to, but he could imagine what its skin would look like in the sun with the light glinting on it.

He swallowed. "I want to trust you," he told Blake— mainly because a dragon as big as a truck was carrying him to an unknown place.

"Then do. Please. I know I didn't give you a reason to trust me until now, but I swear to you that you're safe," Blake begged. He sounded desperate, and even though Sheldon didn't understand why, he'd gotten his brother back, and he wasn't going to protest too much.

Well, outside of being carried by a flying dragon.

He swallowed. "Fine. Let's say I trust you. What's going to happen to me?"

"For now, we're going to land soon and check your wounds. If Hans weren't dead already, I'd go back and kill him myself for what he did to you."

Sheldon was touched by how fierce Blake sounded. "It was kind of my fault. I should have listened to you and stayed away."

"You're right. You should have. We wouldn't be together if you had, though. I missed you."

"So did I. I could have done without the dragons, but I'm happy to see you."

Blake laughed. He looked better now that Sheldon wasn't angry at him. How could Sheldon be? He'd thought he was going to die, but instead, he was flying away, and even though he was terrified, it was also kind of incredible.

"They're my friends," Blake said, looking up.

Sheldon didn't understand how his brother had become friends with dragons, but he doubted he would get an answer to that right now. "How long before we land?"

"A bit. We have to head out of the city and get deeper into the forest. Once we're there, we'll land for the rest of the night. We'll take care of your wounds, and I'll explain everything. Then, the next time we fly, we'll be able to do it on their backs."

Sheldon eyed the other dragons. "How safe is it?" He didn't *feel* safe here, but at least the dragon was holding him steadily. He could imagine how slippery he would be if he was sitting on the dragon's back.

"Don't worry about it. It's not the first time I've done it, and I promise you it's doable. You're safe, Sheldon. Relax and enjoy the experience. Not a lot of people can say they've flown on a dragon."

That much was true. Sheldon looked around again. He didn't like being so high in the air, but there was nothing he could do about it, so he might as well enjoy it.

Sheldon gently put his hands on the huge paw wrapped around him. He felt the dragon shudder, but it's hold didn't loosen, and Sheldon relaxed. He would never have thought he could relax in such a situation, but Blake wasn't wrong. How many people could say they'd flown on a dragon?

Sheldon looked around. The dragons flying around him were giant, and they looked fierce. It was obvious they were used to battle, but they were also beautiful. Their colors were muted in the darkness, but he could see how different they were, and of course, there was no disguising how elegantly and how smoothly they moved. He'd never thought he would see one from this close, let alone five of them.

And he was pretty sure his brother was somehow talking to his dragon. Every time he looked, Blake was staring up and stroking the dragon's paw as if it was a pet. No matter what Blake said about the dragons being his *friends*, Sheldon had a hard time believing it.

He wouldn't get answers anytime soon, so he focused on

what was around him. Not being able to see much was scary, but also amazing. Sheldon was flying. He was leaving his old life behind, albeit in a way he hadn't expected. He'd found his brother.

He was in pain, but all of that had been worth what he was living now.

Morven was relieved when Sheldon finally calmed down and they managed to fly without him screaming and getting the attention of the people under them. The city was asleep, and luckily, they made it out without anyone noticing them, or at least, Morven hoped so. They would find out eventually, but for now, they were in the clear.

Which meant he had to alert the queen, or, since she would probably be sleeping, the next best thing.

He passed on his message to the dragon in charge when he wasn't at the palace, telling her to alert the queen once the queen woke up. Once he'd done that, he started to wonder when they should land. He didn't have a problem carrying Sheldon, but he knew the man could do with some rest, and they needed to check his wounds to make sure they weren't worse than they seemed, especially since they already seemed pretty bad.

How much longer? Orran asked after a while.

Morven looked around. They'd left the city behind, and now the only thing he could see as far as he looked were trees. *Anytime we want, I think. I doubt anyone is following us. Besides, we only have to end the night here. Once Sheldon is rested, we can take flight.*

The next clearing, then.

The next clearing, Morven agreed. They needed space to land. They were used to this kind of landing, though, so he didn't need a lot of it.

Morven was relieved when they finally located one. He

sent Octavia, Hogan, and Slavin first so they could make sure there would be nothing on the ground that could hurt the humans. Morven and Orran couldn't exactly move them around, since they were holding them in their paws, which meant they had to be careful. They weren't used to landing while holding someone, although Orran had more experience than Morven.

Everything is clear. You can land, Octavia said.

Morven looked at Orran. *Tell Blake to alert his brother. I don't want him to freak out again.*

How am I supposed to do that? I can't talk to him in this form.

Morven blinked. He'd almost forgotten that they couldn't communicate with humans when they were dragons. He'd seen Blake and Orran do it, although he supposed that it depended on what they had to tell each other.

Let's go slow, then. That will give them time to understand what's going on.

Orran nodded. Morven turned and focused on his own landing. It wasn't going to be easy with Sheldon now clutching his hand, but he would manage.

He lowered slowly to give Sheldon time to get used to the movement. He was glad when his feet hit the ground, though. He didn't let go of Sheldon right away, afraid he might stumble. To his surprise, Sheldon stayed fairly still. He seemed almost afraid that Morven would hurt him if he didn't, and Morven didn't like that. He didn't want Sheldon to be frightened of him. Sheldon wasn't an enemy, and Morven didn't want him to be one. He wanted the human to be comfortable, just like Blake was.

"You guys stay how you are, all right?" Blake asked.

Not a problem for me, Hogan grumbled. He'd always been the one who had more problems accepting Blake, and he hadn't changed. Still, he was here, which meant that in a way, he did care. Orran lowered his head so he and Blake could look at each other in the eyes. Blake reached out and rubbed

Orran's nose, which made Orran wrinkle it. "I'll tell him everything as soon as possible. I think he'll freak out too much if you shift right now, though."

Sheldon wiggled to get out of Morven's hold, and Morven let him go. He flexed his fingers once the human was free and stared at him.

Sheldon stared back.

He didn't seem to have heard what Blake was telling Orran, which was good. Blake was going to have to find a way to tell his brother that dragons were actually shifters, and Morven was looking forward to listening in on that conversation. He hadn't been there when Blake had found out, and he was curious.

"This is incredible," Sheldon murmured.

He reached for Morven's nose, and Morven jerked back, surprised. Sheldon snatched his hand away, holding against his chest as if he was afraid Morven would bite it. Morven wasn't going to hurt him, though. He'd just been surprised.

Anytime someone had touched him in his dragon form, it had been a dragon. Even Blake stayed away from him as much as he could. The only dragon shifter he touched was Orran, and while Morven was curious about how it felt, he didn't think that finding out now was the best idea.

He huffed and turned to Blake. *What if I wanted to shift?* he asked, but of course, Blake couldn't hear him.

Do what he asks, Orran said.

Morven glared at him. *I thought I was the one in charge today.*

You are, but he's not asking you to stay in your dragon form forever. He only wants a few moments to explain to his brother what's going on. Besides, before you met him, you never shifted to your human form. How is this any different?

It's not. Except, it was. Morven had gotten used to spending more time in his human form, and he wanted to talk to Sheldon. He wanted to make sure the man was okay, but he also wanted to hear what he thought about what was happening.

Blake rushed to his brother, and Morven didn't miss the way Sheldon winced when Blake hugged him. He reached out for Blake and gently pushed him away, and when Blake looked at him, he arched a brow.

Blake chuckled and shook his head. "I don't know what you're doing, but thank you. I don't want to hurt Sheldon more than he already is."

Morven nodded and sat down. He wasn't going anywhere, and he suspected Blake already knew that.

Blake sucked in a breath. "How are you feeling?" he asked Sheldon.

Sheldon looked like he was about to drop on his face, but he stood up straighter. "I'm fine. Now, explain."

"I should check your wounds first."

"You should give me answers first. If you don't, I'm going to freak out again, and we both know you don't want that. No one will hear me scream, but I suspect your dragons won't like it."

Blake sighed. "All right. I'll tell you."

A loud noise made all of them jump, and they turned around to see Octavia and Slavin pawing at each other. They were playing like children, and Morven glared at them. They didn't seem repentant, but at least they stopped trying to knock each other into trees.

Sheldon chuckled breathlessly. "I can't believe any of this."

"You're going to have to. You're also going to have to believe things that sound even more incredible than spending time with five dragons. I swear I'm telling the truth. I will never lie to you."

"Why do I feel like I won't like what you're about to say?"

"I don't know if you'll like it, but I know you'll be surprised."

Sheldon nodded. Morven turned his attention to Octavia. *Since you're playing around, you surely have time to light a fire. The humans have to be cold.* Especially Sheldon, since he was

53

only wearing a thin shirt.

On it, boss.

Morven glared, but there was no heat in it.

"I know Hans told you about the egg I found in his closet," Blake was telling Sheldon.

"You stole it."

"I did. I knew that Hans was going to sell it, and the baby dragon would be hurt. I couldn't allow that to happen, so I stole it and snuck out. I didn't get far before Hans caught me, and these five dragons landed and scared the fuck out of me. Imagine how freaked out I was. One of them landed in front of me, and I thought it was going to eat me. Instead, it became a human and asked me for the egg. I didn't know what was happening, but I refused, and after a while, he turned back into a dragon and grabbed me. We flew away, pretty much like we did today." He reached for Orran, who pushed his nose against Blake's palm.

"You said it became a human?" Sheldon said slowly.

"I did. I swear it's what happened. They're not animals. They're shifters."

"That doesn't make sense."

Blake turned to Morven. "Do you mind shifting?"

Morven grinned at him, which he was sure made him look unhinged, and obeyed. He turned into his human form and stood next to Sheldon with his arms crossed over his chest. Sheldon looked him up and down. Then, his eyelids fluttered, and he fell back.

Sheldon didn't know what happened. One moment, he was standing there, and the next, he felt faint. He didn't know if it was because of the beating he'd taken and his possible concussion, or because the dragon who had made him fly had suddenly turned into a human.

Well, he hadn't been a human exactly. He'd looked kind of

human, but he was still very obviously a dragon. Sheldon's brain couldn't make sense of what he'd seen, and he supposed it had shut down.

When he opened his eyes, it was to see Blake kneeling over him, obviously worried. His eyes widened, and he reached for him. "I'm sorry. I didn't know how else to tell you."

"Having one of them shift in front of me probably wasn't the best idea, considering the rest of my evening." He frowned. "Or maybe it was last night. I can't remember."

"We should check his wounds," someone said.

Blake turned toward them. "You scared him. Stay where you are."

"It's not my fault he got scared. *You* told me to shift."

Sheldon tried to sit up. Blake hadn't been lying. The dragons truly could become human, and from the sound of it, they could talk.

He felt faint again, but he didn't want to pass out. This was too much, and he wasn't sure his brain could process it, but he had to try. "Are we safe?" he asked Blake.

Blake nodded. "I promise. I'm in love with one of them. They won't hurt you."

Sheldon wasn't even surprised. Knowing that Blake was dating a dragon seemed like the most innocuous thing in the entire situation.

"I should check on him," another voice said.

It was still male, and Sheldon blinked, wondering if dragons worked the same way humans did. He associated the tone of voice with a male, but he could be wrong. He didn't want to make the dragons angry, so he leaned closer to Blake. "What are their names?" Maybe that way, he would understand whether the dragons talking to him were males or females.

Blake smiled. "The one who scared you to death is Morven. This other one is Orran, my boyfriend. He's going to help you, so stay still."

Sheldon nodded and leaned back. The ground was hard but still felt better than getting to his feet. He watched as someone came closer, and he realized that another dragon had shifted. This had to be Orran, Blake's boyfriend, because he was blue, just like the dragon who'd carried Blake.

The dragon was strange yet beautiful. Physically, he looked mostly human—he had a head, two arms, and two legs. He also had slitted pupils, bright blue hair, and he was entirely naked. His body was covered in patches of dragon skin that glinted in the light that came from a fire Sheldon hadn't noticed until now.

He kept his gaze firmly above Orran's waist. "I can't say this is how I wanted to meet my brother's boyfriend."

Orran looked surprised, but he smiled. "The same goes for me, but I'm still happy to meet you."

"So am I." Sheldon had dozens of questions, but he didn't want to embarrass anyone. He wanted to ask Blake, but right now, Orran was starting to poke at him, and it wasn't the best moment.

It hurt. There was no other word for it, and Sheldon stayed as still as he could, allowing Orran to work. He hoped the dragon knew what he was doing.

"Well, I can see a few open wounds, and he's going to be bruised," Orran told Blake. Blake had settled at Sheldon's head, and Sheldon was using his legs as a pillow.

"Anything broken?" Blake asked.

Sheldon focused on the two of them. He already knew he was hurt, and he didn't need a laundry list of his wounds. He was interested in the relationship between his brother and Orran, though.

It was obvious they cared for each other. It was in the way they looked at each other and how they leaned closer when they spoke. They were almost like magnets, and Sheldon felt like he was intruding.

"I think at least one rib is broken. It's also possible he has a concussion." Orran turned his attention back to Sheldon. "How are you feeling?"

"Like two men beat me up."

Orran huffed a surprised laugh. "I see. Well, I'll patch you up as well as I can considering the circumstances. Then we can sit around the fire so you can eat and rest. You're freezing, and you're no doubt tired, but you have questions, and you won't sleep until you have answers."

"How do you know?"

"Because that's how your brother is."

Sheldon laughed and regretted it right away. "Don't make me laugh. It hurts."

Orran nodded. "That will be the broken rib. Stay still."

Sheldon obeyed. He hadn't noticed that one of the dragons had carried a small backpack, and he was relieved when he saw the medical supplies inside. He wanted to shower, but he supposed that having someone clean his wounds and bandage them was better than nothing.

He felt nowhere near better once Orran was done with him, and he smiled in relief when Orran handed him a painkiller. "Take this and eat something," he ordered.

"I don't have food."

"We do. If it's not enough, we can hunt something for you."

Sheldon could only imagine a dragon hunting for him. "I'm sure that whatever you have will be enough."

When Sheldon finally got to his feet and headed toward the fire, he saw that another two dragons had shifted. One of them was still in his dragon form, though, curled up next to the fire.

Sheldon leaned against Blake. "Who is that one? Why isn't he shifting?"

"That's Hogan. Don't mind him. I don't think he likes humans very much."

"Is he going to eat me?"

Blake laughed. "None of them are going to eat you. Don't worry about that." He cleared his throat, getting the attention of the dragons. Then, he pointed at them as introduced them. "That's Slavin, then, and Octavia. You already know Orran, of course, and the last one is Morven. He's the team leader. Everyone, this is my brother, Sheldon."

Sheldon shuffled his feet. "Thanks for coming for me," he said. He knew that even though Orran was dating his brother, the other dragons hadn't had a reason to help him.

"Don't worry about it," Octavia said. She was smiling, and it helped Sheldon relax. The fact that she was a bit more shapely than the other two dragons in human form helped identify her as female, and Sheldon felt less unsettled.

He lowered himself to the ground, as close as to the fire as he could without burning himself. He was surprised when Blake handed him a sandwich, but he accepted it with a smile.

He needed this. Even though he was still in pain, he was warm, was about to eat, and more importantly, he was with his brother.

"So you can turn into humans," he said.

Morven snorted. "You have an exceptional power of observation."

"Don't make fun of him," Blake snapped.

"I don't mind it," Sheldon said. "I have many questions, but I don't think I have the strength to listen to the answers now."

He was pretty sure Morven mumbled something that sounded like *thank the sky*, but he ignored him. Now that he was with his brother, he could relax. He ate, and as soon as he was done, his eyes started to close. He wanted to stay awake and ask his questions, but he hadn't been lying. He didn't have the strength.

"Go to sleep," Blake murmured. "We'll still be here tomorrow, and we'll answer any question you have."

Sheldon nodded and leaned against his brother. Blake wrapped an arm around his shoulders and squeezed, and Sheldon smiled.

He wasn't home, but he was home away from home with Blake. That was all that mattered right now.

Chapter Four

When Sheldon woke up the next morning, he was still worried. It was a mix of being in pain, not knowing what was going to happen next, and having to wrap his mind around everything he'd learned last night.

He still couldn't believe it. Dragons could become humans, and they looked incredible. It wasn't even because they were gorgeous, at least not entirely. They were *fascinating*, and Sheldon wanted to ask how it worked—how they could shift, how they decided which form they wanted to be in.

He kept his mouth shut, though. When he woke up, he found the dragon still in his dragon form, staring at him. He was close enough to be able to nibble on Sheldon's toes, and Sheldon slowly folded his legs so that he could put some distance between them. The dragon huffed and moved away, but not before Sheldon saw what he thought was a smile.

Sheldon was pretty sure he was still asleep and dreaming.

"How are you feeling this morning?" a voice asked.

Sheldon jerked, his heart racing with panic and pain. He saw it was only Orran, Blake's boyfriend, and he relaxed.

"I'm sorry I scared you," Orran said.

"Don't worry about it. After being kidnapped and beaten, I think I'm going to be jumpy for a bit."

Orran nodded and crouched next to Sheldon. "How are you feeling?" he asked again.

"I've been better, but I'll be fine."

Orran nodded and handed a packet to Sheldon. When Sheldon opened it, he found a second sandwich. "Thank you," he told Orran.

"You're welcome. You should eat. As soon as you're ready, we'll shift back and head home."

"Where is home?" Sheldon asked before biting into the sandwich. He'd always imagined dragons lived in caverns, but now that he knew they weren't animals, he wondered.

"We live in a palace dug into a mountain."

Sheldon blinked. Had he heard that right? "A palace?"

"The queen will want to meet you. She agreed to let us rescue you, but she'll want to make sure you not a danger to the clan."

All right, so maybe Sheldon should have asked at least some of the questions he had yesterday. Still, now that Orran had told him that tidbit of information, he had enough things to think about for a bit.

Dragons had a queen. Apparently, they lived in clans. They also lived in a mountain, whatever that meant.

He ate, peeking at the dragons around him. Four of them were still in their human form, and they were close together, talking to each other. Sheldon's gaze settled on Morven, who Blake had told him was the leader. Now that it was day, Sheldon could see him more clearly, and he was impressed.

He knew that Morven was the dragon who had carried him. He was the only green one, so it was kind of obvious. He thought Morven was gorgeous in his dragon form, but the same went for his human one. The daylight caught on the patches of dragon skin on his body, making them gleam. All the dragons were naked, just like the night before, which reminded Sheldon that he wanted to ask Blake about it.

"Why are they naked?" he asked, leaning closer to his brother, who was just waking up.

Blake rubbed his eyes. "What?"

"The dragons. Why are they naked?"

Blake chuckled. "That's what I asked the second time

Orran shifted in front of me. To make a long answer short, they're naked because they're not used to being in their human forms. Usually, they stay in their dragon ones. They don't need clothes when they're dragons. They don't understand the need for them."

"It's kind of hard not to stare."

"I know. They won't be offended if you do, though. They don't see the world the way we do."

"I have so many questions."

"I'll give you as many answers as I can, but I know they'll want to fly out soon, so you should focus on eating."

Sheldon did just that. Blake was right. He needed his strength to fly, since he'd be riding a dragon, and he didn't want to fall once they were in the air.

Things went well until they had to fly again. Blake had told Sheldon they would sit on the back of the dragons, but not that he *had* to do it. He couldn't help but wonder if it was disrespectful. He looked at Morven, already in his dragon form and standing in front of him, then back at Blake. "Are you sure I should do this? I don't want to treat him like an animal."

Blake nodded. "It's the most comfortable way to fly with them. Trust me. I've been doing this for a while now."

"Still. It's weird. I don't want to be disrespectful."

Morven huffed and shifted back to his human form. He stood there in front of Sheldon, and Sheldon had to look away.

Morven was fascinating. Sheldon wanted to stare, but he didn't want to offend anyone. He also couldn't help but stare at Blake and Orran. They were affectionate with each other, and Blake didn't seem to see the differences between them. He didn't have any reaction to Orran's body, probably because he was used to it, but it was still strange.

"You won't be disrespectful if you ride me," Morven said.

Sheldon's cheeks heated. He knew Morven hadn't meant it in a sexual way, but that was where his mind had gone.

Okay, so maybe he wasn't as weirded out by Morven as he'd thought. Maybe he found Morven attractive. That didn't mean he was going to sleep with the dragon. He didn't even know how that would work. "I just want to make sure you know I don't see you like an animal," he explained.

"I know I'm not an animal. I know you don't think that. We have to start flying, though. I can carry you in my hand if you want me to, but this would be easier and safest."

Sheldon hesitated, but he gave Morven the only answer he could. "All right. I'll ride you." He made sure not to look at Morven when he said that.

Morven nodded and shifted back. Once he was in his dragon form again, Sheldon looked at him. "How am I supposed to do it, though?"

"I can help you on Morven's back, or he can. You just have to climb up and find a comfortable place you can hold on to as he flies," Blake explained.

Morven looked like a small mountain in front of Sheldon, but it wasn't like Sheldon had any other choices, so he nodded and went to work.

His ribs hurt as he climbed, and he bit his lower lip so he wouldn't cry out. He was pretty sure he'd irritated Morven yesterday when he'd done all that screaming, and he didn't want to make things worse.

It wasn't easy to find a comfortable spot on Morven's back. The dragon's skin was hard and smooth, making it almost impossible to find a place where Sheldon wouldn't slip. In the end, he settled himself between two hard ridges on Morven's back. That way, he wouldn't slide down Morven's back too much, and he had something to hold on to. Sliding sideways was going to be another problem, but Sheldon supposed he was going to find out how big of a problem it was soon.

He looked down at Blake. "I'm settled."

Blake nodded. "Good. Hold on tight."

When he climbed onto Orran's back, he was much faster than Sheldon, and he seemed to know the exact spot where he should sit down. He leaned closer to Orran, gently patting his skin and talking to him. Sheldon didn't have more time to stare, though, because Morven moved under him. Sheldon squeaked, but before he could be afraid, they were already in the air.

It was cold, but it was also incredible, and Sheldon closed his eyes and smiled.

Morven felt Sheldon settle on his back as they flew. He'd been agitated in the beginning, holding onto Morven to the point of pain. Morven hadn't protested because one, he wouldn't have been able to in his dragon form, and two, he wanted Sheldon to feel as safe as possible. He realized it would be hard considering Sheldon had never ridden a dragon, so he was glad when he felt the hold Sheldon had on his back loosen. He never let go, thankfully, but Morven thought he was enjoying the flight more than he was afraid of it now.

Morven flew close to Orran so the brothers could talk to each other if they felt like it, but they were silent. From what he could see, Blake was talking to Orran, even though Orran couldn't answer. As for Sheldon, now that he was relaxing, he was keeping up an endless stream of chatter.

"I still can't believe he didn't tell me about you guys," he grumbled.

Morven didn't have to ask to know who he was talking about. He was amused by how Sheldon seemed to hold a grudge against his brother. Sheldon understood why Blake hadn't told him about Orran and the others, but he didn't sound like he liked it.

"If he had, I wouldn't have gone to the bar. I wouldn't have been beaten up, and I wouldn't be in pain," Sheldon continued. "I also wouldn't be bloody. I mean, Orran tried to clean me up, but he could only do so much. Now I'm going to be introduced to your queen all bloody. It's already bad enough that I'm in pain and freaking out. I could at least make the best impression, but no. I look a mess."

Morven grumbled with laughter, his sides moving. Sheldon yelped and grabbed the spurs on Morven's back harder.

"It's not funny," he snapped.

Morven wasn't surprised he understood that Morven was laughing, but it wasn't at him. For whatever reason, he found Sheldon kind of adorable. Now that Sheldon was over the fear, he seemed like a nice person, and he was cute.

"I mean it. Do you think it would be possible for me to take a shower or something like that before I meet the queen? I don't want her to think I stink."

Morven eyed the lake they were passing over. They were almost at the palace, and while he knew Sheldon would be given time to clean up before meeting the queen, he had an idea. He looked over his shoulder, and Sheldon looked back, his eyes wide.

"What are you doing? Shouldn't you be looking ahead since we're flying? Are we going to crash?" Morven grinned, and Sheldon's eyes went even rounder. "I'm not kidding. What are you planning?"

Morven dove. Sheldon screeched, and Morven felt him scramble to grab onto something. It didn't take them long to hit the water, though, and they slid into the lake, Sheldon's screams fading. Morven grinned again, and when he felt Sheldon slip off his back, he turned around to look at him. He wanted to refresh Sheldon and play around with him, not to drown him, so he made sure Sheldon could swim and that he was able to stay at the surface. Sheldon was flailing and trying to get his head out of the water, and Morven remembered too late that his ribs were possibly broken.

He was an idiot.

He shifted to his human form and quickly swam toward Sheldon. Once he was there, he wrapped an arm around Sheldon's waist and held him close. Then he propelled them to the surface. Sheldon clung to him, wrapping himself around him, but it wasn't a problem for Morven. He was used to swimming, and Sheldon wouldn't stop him.

They broke the surface. Sheldon spluttered while Morven smiled at him.

Sheldon slapped Morven's shoulder, but he didn't let go of him. "What did you think you were doing?" he asked.

Morven grinned. "You were complaining that you were all bloody. You wanted to clean up, so here we are."

"You thought that me wanting to clean up meant I wanted to take a dip in a frozen lake?"

"It's not frozen."

"It's certainly not warm."

Morven tightened his hold around Sheldon. "I'll keep you warm."

Sheldon spluttered and stared at Morven. "I don't even know what to say." His gaze flicked down to Morven's chest. "You're naked."

"I am." Morven wasn't ashamed of it. He didn't own clothes. He didn't understand them, although since humans were different, they probably needed clothes to keep them warm.

Sheldon tried to push away. Morven kept his hold on him.

"What are you doing?" Sheldon asked.

"I can't let you go until I'm sure you won't drown."

Sheldon glared. His cheeks were red, and somehow, it made him even cuter. It didn't even matter that one of his eyes was swollen and he was starting to bruise. Morven knew that once Sheldon was healed, he would be stunning.

He looked kind of like Blake, yet not. Blake's jaw was squarer, and his entire face looked harder. Sheldon was soft, and Morven wanted to touch him.

"I can swim."

Morven blinked. "Are you sure?"

"I'm sure. I'm in pain, which is what's holding me back, not the fact that I can't swim."

"I apologize. I should have thought better before doing this."

"To me, it looks like you didn't think at all."

Sheldon shivered, and Morven pulled him closer. He wanted to share his body warmth with Sheldon, since what was happening was entirely his fault. To his surprise, Sheldon didn't push him away. Instead, he leaned into him, and Morven couldn't help but smile.

"Let me take you to the shore. You don't even have to swim. I'll do all the work."

Sheldon eyed Morven. "I won't have to move a muscle?"

"You won't."

"Do you have to shift back?"

Morven pressed his lips together. "Not if you don't want me to."

Sheldon looked away. "I didn't say anything about not wanting you to shift, but you're warm."

"I'll stay in this form, then."

Morven started to swim. Sheldon was clinging to him, and while it was a bit of a bother, he didn't say anything about it. It was his fault Sheldon was in this situation, and while he didn't regret it because he thought Sheldon had fun, no matter how much he was complaining, he should have thought better of it.

Sheldon was injured. He needed a healer and rest. What he *didn't* need was a dunk in the lake.

When they got to the shore, Morven saw that the others had landed and were waiting for them there. Orran had shifted, while the other three had stayed in their dragon form. Hogan rolled his eyes at Morven, but Morven ignored him and focused on Sheldon, who was shivering even harder and dripping.

Blake stood there, his arms crossed over his chest, glaring at Morven. "What did you think you were doing? He's got to be freezing, and we don't have a change of clothes for him."

Orran put a hand on Blake's shoulder. "We'll get him dry. Don't worry. We're dragons, after all."

Blake shook his head. "Sheldon could have been hurt."

To Morven's surprise, Sheldon stepped forward to defend him. "But I wasn't. I won't deny it probably wasn't the best idea, but I'm kind of glad Morven did it. I needed a moment before getting to the palace."

Blake stared at him before nodding. "All right. You're going to have to strip."

Sheldon's cheeks blazed. "Naked?" he asked in a strangled voice.

Blake smirked. "Is there another way to strip?"

"We promise we won't stare," Orran said.

Sheldon sighed. "I suppose there's no way around this. Fine. But you better keep me warm while I'm naked."

Somehow, Morven suspected that the words were for him rather than Orran. He wasn't going to ask, though. Sheldon seemed to be more comfortable with him today, and he wanted that to continue. He didn't understand why he felt protective of Sheldon, although he wanted to attribute it to Sheldon being human and wounded. He needed to be protected. Orran was already focused on Blake, and Morven didn't have a problem focusing on Sheldon.

Sheldon was nervous as they neared the palace. He almost wanted to go back to the lake, even though he'd been half-frozen and dripping wet once he got out.

He'd also been flustered.

He still wasn't sure what had possessed Morven to take a dip in the lake, although he didn't regret it. He'd been obsessing over the queen and what she was going to tell him, and it had been a nice distraction. Now, though, distractions were over, and he was about to meet the queen.

Was she going to ask him to leave? He wasn't sure how he could stay, not when Blake had made it clear that the only reason he was allowed to was that he was the queen's son's tutor.

And wasn't that incredible? Blake, who hadn't been able to keep a job longer than a few months, was a teacher. He was a teacher to a *baby dragon*.

What had Sheldon's life become?

Sheldon didn't know what he would be allowed to do, but he also didn't know what he *wanted* to do. His life was back in the city. That was where his job was, as well as his parents.

Blake was here, though. Even if that was the only reason for Sheldon to stay, it made him want to do just that.

He didn't think he would be allowed to, so he tried not to keep his hopes up as the dragons neared a mountain. In the beginning, he hadn't noticed anything strange about it, but as they moved closer, he finally noticed the openings in it. They looked like caves from a distance, but now he could see they were windows.

He had no idea what to expect. Blake had said the dragons lived in a palace, but Sheldon's mind had gone to something rustic, with a lot of stone, wood, and other natural construction materials. It looked like he was right when the dragons flew into the mountain from the top, landing on a wide slab of stone. The walls were simple stone, too, and it was somewhat disappointing.

Sheldon slid off Morven's back and looked around, wondering where the queen was.

"How are you doing?" Blake asked as soon as he was off Orran.

"I think I'll be better once I've had some rest, but I'm fine."

Blake stared, clearly not convinced. "You don't have to be strong. You can tell me if you're in pain or if you need anything, especially after the stunt Morven pulled. I don't understand why he did that."

"I already explained myself," Morven said. His voice wasn't harsh, but he didn't sound pleased, either.

"And I already told you I'm fine," Sheldon said before Blake and Morven could start fighting.

They were both protective of Sheldon, something Sheldon didn't understand. For Blake, it made sense. For Morven, not at all. Still, he couldn't deny the obvious.

Morven had thought it would be fun for them to take a swim, and he hadn't been wrong. Sheldon had been so worried about what was happening that he'd been obsessing. The dip in the lake had been a distraction. It would have been even better if he hadn't been in pain, but he didn't blame Morven. It had helped him relax, and now he felt he was ready to meet the queen.

Mostly.

"I'll let the healer confirm that," Blake said.

"There's a doctor here?"

"What do you think we are? Savages?" Morven asked.

Sheldon wasn't sure if Morven was serious or if he was playing around. "I'm sorry. That's not what I meant."

Morven smiled. "I know. We might be dragons, but it doesn't mean we don't have modern comforts. You'll see."

"And you should head to the queen to tell her about the mission," Octavia said.

Morven groaned. "Do I really have to?"

"You're the team leader and head of security for the clan. I'm pretty sure you do." She grinned. "Blake and Orran will take care of Sheldon."

"We will," Blake confirmed.

Was it going to become a pissing context between Blake and Morven? Sheldon didn't have the energy to focus on that, but he knew that if he had, he would find it amusing. "I don't care who takes care of me as long as I can sleep for a bit and eat. I also wouldn't mind a shower with soap."

"You already had a bath," Morven pointed out.

"It was cold, and now I smell like the lake." But at least he was warm-ish. His clothes had been steaming after the dragons dried them, but all the warmth had vanished as soon as Morven was in the air again.

Morven leaned closer and took a sniff. Sheldon felt his entire body go up in flames. He knew his cheeks were red when Morven leaned back, and that Morven had noticed. "You don't stink," Morven declared.

"Really? Thank you so much. Now I can avoid showering."

"You can take a bath and eat all you want once we're back to our rooms," Blake intervened.

Sheldon resisted the urge to slap his brother on the back of the head for interrupting whatever had been happening between him and Morven. "Thank you." He turned back to Morven. "Will I see you again?"

Morven looked amused. "Do you *want* to see me again?"

"Of course not. I don't like you."

From the way Morven was still smiling, Sheldon knew he didn't believe him. Good, because Sheldon had been lying.

"I'll see you around. I'm head of security. I have to stick my nose into new people's business, especially humans. Besides, I'll be there when you meet the queen." He paused and gently touched Sheldon's cheekbone. "Go with your brother.

71

He and Orran will take care of you. You need some rest and a healer."

"Thank you," Sheldon said. There was nothing else he could say, even though he wished there was. Morven confused him, but in the best of ways.

Morven nodded and stepped away. "All right. Take him to your rooms. Get the healer and make sure he has everything he needs. The queen will understand if he's not up to meeting her right now, but she'll probably want to later today or tomorrow."

"We'll take care of him," Orran confirmed.

"I have to go to the queen." Morven paused. "You sure you don't want your old job back?"

Orran laughed. "Never."

Morven and the other three dragons left, while Sheldon stayed with Orran and Blake. He wouldn't have minded riding Morven, especially once they passed through an opening in the stone wall and he saw how massive the palace was.

What had he expected? They were inside a mountain.

It looked like the dragons had dug all the way into the mountain and created their palace there. The hallways were wide enough that two dragons could pass each other without even touching. Sheldon knew his eyes were huge as he tried taking everything in, but his head was spinning.

He was relieved when Blake reached for him. "You look like you're about to fall flat on your face."

"I feel like it, too," Sheldon confessed.

"We should have asked Morven to take you to our rooms before he left. Orran can shift and carry you."

"How far is your room?" Sheldon didn't want to ride Orran. It would feel like a betrayal, even though he knew it was ridiculous. Still, Orran was Blake's boyfriend, and Sheldon didn't want to encroach.

"About ten minutes?"

"I can walk."

Or at least, he thought so until they reached the center of the mountain. Ramps lined the walls, and dragons were walking up and down them as well as flying in the empty center of the room. Sheldon swallowed, both in awe, and terrified at the thought that he was going to have to climb or go down those ramps.

"I'll shift," Orran said.

"I'm sorry."

Orran smiled softly. "Don't be. You're injured."

"Because I was an idiot."

"Because you care about your brother and you wanted to make sure he was safe." He didn't add anything. Instead, he shifted, and Blake helped Sheldon climb onto his back.

It was the same, yet different. Sheldon was tenser on Orran's back, and he tried not to touch too much. Luckily for him, Orran didn't take flight. Instead, he slowly walked down a ramp, Blake walking next to him.

"It's going to take you some time to get used to all of this," Blake said. "The palace is huge, because it was built for dragons."

"That was kind of obvious."

Blake rolled his eyes.

Sheldon was pretty sure he dozed off during the ten minutes it took them to get to Blake and Orran's room. He opened his eyes when he felt Orran stop, and he saw they were standing in front of a wide door. Blake helped him slide off, and when Orran shifted back, he opened the door.

Sheldon hadn't even thought that dragons might sleep in nests. He'd expected a bedroom, and it was. There wasn't a bed in it, though.

The nest was made of soft-looking fabrics—a lot of them. Sheldon looked away, knowing that his brother and Orran shared the nest.

"We have a small guest room," Blake said as he moved toward the side of the room. Sheldon hadn't noticed the door there, but he followed his brother. It opened on a short but wide hallway. There were two doors, and Blake pushed open one of them. "This is the guest room." He rubbed the back of his neck. "I'm sorry there's no bed. You'll have to get used to nests."

"It's fine."

"I'll find you some clothes. It's probably going to have to be mine, but they'll fit."

"They'll be huge." Not only was Blake taller, but he was also wider. He was muscled, while Sheldon had always been on the scrawny side.

Blake grinned. "You have to get used to things being huge, too. Everything is big here." He pushed open the second door. "See? That's the bath."

It looked more like a pool, which Sheldon supposed made sense, since it was built for a dragon. "How much does it cost to fill it?"

"You don't have to think about any of that. Don't worry. I'll take care of you, and you don't have to repay me or anything like that. I'm pretty sure the dragons would be offended if you tried to. Focus on healing and getting better. We can talk about everything else later."

Sheldon nodded. He wanted nothing more than to bathe and sleep, and since Blake was offering, he wouldn't say no to either.

Morven shifted back once he left the landing pad. Octavia snickered behind him, but he didn't turn to look at her. He knew the other three were in their dragon form, too, as they headed toward the throne room. The queen would already know they were back, and she'd want news about Sheldon and the situation they'd walked in.

You like him, Octavia said.

I have no idea what you're talking about.

Sure you don't.

Morven didn't bother to look at her. *The three of you should get some rest, too.*

Is that an order? Slavin asked.

It is. Get out of my sight. If he could, Morven would join them. He'd never really thought about what being the head of security would mean when it came to his friends. They weren't merely his team members. They were his family, and he wanted to spend time with them. He wanted them to unwind from the mission by eating and talking together. Instead, he had to meet the queen.

She was waiting for him when he got to the throne room. The guards nodded at him when he walked into the room, and they closed the door behind him.

How is he? the queen asked.

Morven walked closer to the throne. *He's going to need a healer.*

What happened?

The people holding him hostage beat him up. Orran thinks he has at least one broken rib, and his face is swollen. He'll live, though.

The queen nodded. *What do you think of him?*

Morven paused to think about it. He liked Sheldon, but he wasn't sure if it was because of how new Sheldon was or because of something else. *He doesn't seem like a bad person. I don't know him well, but he was looking for his brother, and even though he knew he would probably get hurt in the process, that didn't stop him. He's having a hard time wrapping his mind around dragons being shifters, but he was never rude. He was frightened in the beginning, but he's already coming around, and he would be a good addition to the clan.*

The queen arched a brow. *I never mentioned adding him to the clan.*

Dammit. *I apologize. I didn't mean to imply anything.*

The queen stared, and Morven looked away. *I wouldn't be opposed to having another human in the clan*, she finally said.

Morven swallowed. He wanted to ask her about it, but he knew she was going to tell him. He might only be head of security, but she trusted him.

I think it would be a good thing. I want the dragons to see that not all humans are bad. It's why I insisted that Blake become a tutor for Blue. I'm worried about allowing another human in the clan, though. I'd have to meet Sheldon first, but there are also the elders. It was hard enough when I welcomed Blake into the clan. They're going to be outraged when they find out about Sheldon.

Morven knew it was a legitimate worry. Things hadn't been going well, and while the queen was right that Blake was only a catalyst, it didn't make things easier.

We don't even know for sure that he'll want to stay, he pointed out.

From what I know about Blake and his family, I suspect that will be the case. It might take Sheldon some time, but he'll come to see that the palace can be his home.

Only if you allow it.

The queen nodded. *I want to meet him. If I like him, I'll seriously consider adding him to the clan. It's going to take work, though.*

Morven hesitated. He wanted to ask her why she was doing it, but he wasn't sure how she would take the question.

Speak, she said.

Morven should have known she would realize he was holding something back. *Why are you doing this? Why are you allowing humans into the clan?*

Because I think that humans and dragons can live together peacefully.

Morven seriously doubted that, but he didn't say it out loud.

They did once, the queen continued. *Then, humans became*

greedy, and they started killing dragons. It was only a small number of humans, though. There are millions of them on this earth, and most of them like dragons. The fact that a handful of humans kill us and earn money from our hides doesn't change that fact. I want my son to be king in a different world. I want him to understand this.

Morven nodded. *It won't be easy. Like you said, the elders won't be happy about it. We've been staying away from humans, and the elders still see all of them as the enemy.*

But they're not. Blake isn't our enemy, and I don't think Sheldon is, either. I don't know if my hope of humans and dragons living together in peace will ever happen, but even if the world stays the way it is, it doesn't mean we can't have more humans in the clan. I trust Blake, and I want Sheldon to be just as trustworthy.

Morven thought he was. He wasn't the one making decisions, though, so he limited himself to nod. *Are you planning on meeting him today?*

If possible. I'll talk to the healer when he's done with Sheldon. Once I know what's going on with him, I can make decisions. Do you think he would be a good fit with us?

Morven took his time answering that question. He wanted to say yes, but he didn't want to lie.

He liked Sheldon. There was no way to ignore that, even though he didn't know how it had happened. It was what it was, though, and Morven wouldn't mind seeing more of Sheldon. He didn't even know if Sheldon could bring anything to the clan. Blake was Blue's tutor, but what would Sheldon do? *He would be*, he confirmed.

That's what I thought. Blake would be happy to have his brother with him.

Sheldon can't be a tutor, though.

I'm sure we can find him something to do if he decides to stay. We don't have to make this kind of decision right now, though. I have work to do, and you should go back to your duties. I'll make sure the healer contacts you, too. I want you to be there when I meet Sheldon.

I would be honored.

Morven wanted Sheldon to stay. He couldn't ignore that, and he didn't want to, even though he didn't understand why he felt that way.

Chapter Five

Sheldon had been lucky not to have to meet the queen right away. Morven had told him he would, but instead, the healer had prescribed an entire day of rest and healing. Sheldon had tried to protest—he didn't like being at the palace without meeting the queen—but he was also relieved.

He'd wanted time to wrap his mind around everything that was happening. He had his brother again, but it was obvious that Blake wasn't coming back to the city, and Sheldon didn't know what to do with that. If Blake wasn't coming back, what was Sheldon going to do?

There was no doubt in his mind that Blake would stay with Orran. He was happy. Sheldon had observed him all day yesterday, and it was obvious he felt at home with the dragons. Things could be different outside of Orran's rooms, but Sheldon doubted that was the case. Blake had found a place where he belonged. No matter how much it hurt, Sheldon knew that wasn't him anymore.

"You shouldn't be nervous about meeting the queen," Blake said.

Sheldon smiled. Even though he hadn't been thinking about the queen, his brother was right. "She's royalty."

"She won't hurt you, if that's what you're thinking."

"I wasn't, but I've never met a queen."

"She's just like the other dragons."

Somehow, Sheldon doubted it. "Do you think she'll want me to leave right away?"

Blake frowned. "I hope she won't. She agreed to have the

healer see you, so that's good. She's having problems, though, and having a second human here isn't going to make things easy on her."

Blake had tried to explain about the queen and the people trying to use his presence with the clan to get her off the throne, but Sheldon had been in pain, and he'd only half listened. Now, he wished he'd paid more attention.

He wanted to know if someone was going to attack him. It wouldn't change anything, since they were all dragons, and they could eat him with one bite . . . but still. He was touched that the queen had agreed to have him stay even though his presence would complicate her life. He would leave, if that was what she wanted. He *should* leave.

He'd been able to call work from Blake's cell phone this morning. He'd told them he was sick and that he was taking a few days off, but it wouldn't be enough. He didn't want to leave Blake. At the same time, though, he wanted to go home to his familiar life. He wanted his routine back.

He was also fascinated. The palace was vast and beautiful, and the dragons were all gorgeous. Some of them seemed to go out of their way to avoid Sheldon, but several had made a point of crossing his path and nodding at him. He was confused, but it was obvious who wanted him there and who didn't.

Today was no different. The walk through the palace had been short yesterday, but now he was headed to the throne room. He wasn't alone, either. Blake and Orran were there, of course, but so were Octavia, Slavin, and Hogan. Sheldon was surprised at the last one. He'd thought Hogan hated him and all humans, but the fact that he was here to support Sheldon pointed to the contrary. Sheldon was touched, but he knew better than to say anything to Hogan. He'd probably burn him to a crisp.

Morven was waiting for them when they got to the throne

room. There was no mistaking that this was the door they were looking for, either. It was made of wood, with golden designs, and massive, much bigger than any other door Sheldon had seen in the palace. It was imposing, although Sheldon supposed that was the case especially for him, since he was human and much smaller than a dragon.

"Ready?" Blake asked.

Sheldon shook his head. "I don't think I'll ever be ready." Sheldon was intimidated, even though Blake had tried to reassure him.

"You'll be fine."

Sheldon was surprised to hear Morven's voice. He'd been in his dragon form when they'd arrived, and Sheldon thought he would say that way. Instead, he'd shifted, and he was standing behind Sheldon.

Sheldon turned to him. "How can you know that?"

"The queen is a good leader. She won't hurt you. Even if it goes badly, the only thing she'll do is ask you to go home."

Sheldon supposed that was better than eating him.

He took a deep breath and faced the doors. The guards moved to open them. Sheldon jerked when a hand landed on his shoulder, and his eyes widened when he turned around to see that it belonged to Morven. Morven gave him a quick squeeze, then the doors were open, and Sheldon stepped into the throne room.

It was nothing like he'd expected. When he thought of a throne room, his mind went to human royalty. He should have known better, though.

The throne was made of stone, but it wasn't a chair. It looked more like a lounger, and a dragon was sitting on it. There was no doubt in Sheldon's mind that it was the queen.

She was blue, although not the deep blue of Orran. She was lighter, and beautiful. Her gaze landed on Sheldon, and he held his breath.

The queen rose from the throne. She stepped closer, shifting as she moved. It was impressively smooth. When she stopped in front of Sheldon, she was in her human form, and Sheldon made sure to keep his gaze on her face. She was naked, too, and obviously, it was something Sheldon would have to get used to.

"Welcome," the queen said.

Sheldon lightly bowed his head. "Thank you for allowing me to stay with you."

"I wouldn't have had it any other way. You were trying to save your brother, which in my book, is admirable."

Sheldon realized that the queen hadn't had to send dragons to save him. A lot of people probably wouldn't have. He was human, and she didn't know him. He was Blake's brother, but to her, that didn't mean anything. The fact that she'd agreed to have not only Blake rescue him, but also an entire team of dragons, pointed to her being a good person.

Sheldon hoped that was true.

"How are you feeling?" she asked.

"A little banged up. I'll be fine, though."

"I'd offer you a seat, but as you can see, there's only one in this room. We can go to my office to talk."

"It's not a problem." It kind of was. Just like Orran had thought, two of Sheldon's ribs were broken. It hurt every time he breathed. Being on his feet didn't help, but he didn't want to be disrespectful. At least he didn't have a concussion.

"I insist. This was the right way to meet you, but now that we've introduced ourselves, we can be in a more relaxed setting." She looked at the people surrounding Sheldon. "Of course, Orran and Blake are welcome to come with us, as is Morven. I don't think we need the others, though." She arched a brow, obviously amused. "It's almost as if they thought I was going to kick you out."

Sheldon hadn't thought about it like that, but maybe he

should have. He barely knew the dragons, though. He didn't understand why they would want him to stick around.

Octavia, Hogan, and Slavin left the throne room, while everyone else headed toward the back. There was a door there, and while it was smaller than the one that led into the throne room, it was big enough for a dragon to walk through it.

It opened into a wide office that was different from what Sheldon was used to. There was a desk, but no computer on it. There were a lot of books and scrolls on the shelves behind it, and the chair was big enough for a dragon to sit comfortably.

That wasn't where the queen went, though. Instead of heading for her desk, she turned and made her way to an area under a window, where a small table that held glasses and food and chairs meant for humans waited.

Sheldon blinked. "I hope I didn't interrupt your meal," he said.

The queen smiled at him. "You haven't. This is for all of us while we talk. Why don't you have a seat?"

It was obvious to Morven that Sheldon was wary and worried. He wanted to tell Sheldon that he didn't have to be, but he couldn't betray the queen. She'd confided in him that she wanted Sheldon to stay, but neither of them knew whether or not it would work. Sheldon wasn't like Blake. He probably had a life to go back to in the city, which meant he might only here for a short while, probably only the time to heal.

That didn't sit well with Morven.

He'd already accepted the fact that he was fascinated with Sheldon. He hadn't thought he could feel that way for a human, especially since he hadn't when it came to Blake. Now, he realized how stupid he'd been.

He didn't like all dragons. He wasn't attracted to all

dragons. It would make sense that he wasn't attracted to all humans, either.

He *was* attracted to Sheldon, though. There was no denying that. He didn't know what to do with those feelings, and for now, he knew there was nothing he *should* do. He had to focus on Sheldon and on making sure he was okay and that he felt safe. Anything else would come later.

Sheldon lowered himself into one of the chairs. No one missed his grimace, and Blake tried to help him, but Sheldon shook his head.

Once they were all seated—with Morven taking one of the spots next to Sheldon—the queen turned to Sheldon again. "I'm glad to hear you'll heal without lasting injuries."

"It's what the healer says, and I hope he's not lying."

The queen smiled. "He's not. I know you don't have any reasons to trust us, but we're not trying to hurt you."

"I know. I apologize."

"You have nothing to apologize for. I can understand how confused you are. You went from believing that dragons were animals to knowing that's not the case. You were beaten, and you were worried about your brother. It's perfectly under-standable that you're having a hard time wrapping your mind around all of this."

"It's not the easiest thing I've ever done," Sheldon agreed.

The queen nodded. "I hope it will help you to know that I don't have anything against you staying with Blake. You're welcome to stay for as long as you want, even indefinitely, if it's what you desire."

Sheldon blinked at her. Morven held his breath. He hadn't known the queen would make the proposal today. She'd had meetings after they talked yesterday, but he hadn't realized that she'd made her decision.

"I don't know what I want," Sheldon said. "I'm glad to see my brother is fine, but I have a life and a job in the city."

"And you'd like to go back to those?" the queen asked.

"I don't know. I feel like I *should* go back to them."

"Because it's your duty."

"I suppose."

"Well, my offer is on the table. You can stay for a few days or longer. Take the time to heal and to explore the palace and meet the dragons who live here." She hesitated. "I would suggest not to go anywhere on your own, though. It would be easy for you to get lost."

She wasn't telling Sheldon everything. Yes, it would be easy for Sheldon to get lost, but more importantly, it would be easy for a dragon to attack him if he was alone.

Morven wouldn't allow that to happen. He was going to keep an eye on Sheldon and Blake. They were close to the queen through Blue, and they were her guests. Blake was part of the clan now, but a lot of dragons didn't consider it official. Morven wouldn't put it past some of them to try to get rid of him. It would be an offense against the queen, but they were easy targets. They could get hurt, or worse, and no one would know what had happened to them.

"I'm grateful for your offer," Sheldon said. "And I'm definitely going to stay for a bit. I don't think I could face another dragon ride to the city, not in the state I'm in right now."

"Take a few days. Hopefully, by the time you'll feel better, you'll have an answer for me."

"Why do you want me to stay?" Sheldon blurted out.

Luckily, the queen didn't look offended. "Why *wouldn't* I want you to stay?"

"I'm not a dragon."

"But you're Blake's brother. I know Blake, and he's a good person. My son loves him. He saved my baby when no one else would, and I'll always owe him a lot. I suppose this is one of the ways I can thank him for it. I can offer his brother a safe place to stay with us, and if you want, a permanent place with the clan."

"I don't know what to say. Thank you."

"Let me know as soon as you've made your decision. As I'm sure you're already aware, some people won't be happy with your presence here. It's something you have to consider. We'll keep you safe if you decide to stay. I won't allow anyone to hurt my guests or any of my clan members."

"It's a lot to think about." And Sheldon looked over-whelmed as it was.

The queen got to her feet. To everyone's surprise, she reached for Sheldon and cupped his cheek. "You're hurt. You went through a lot, and you're overwhelmed. Take your time. I'm not demanding an answer right now. I want you to decide to stay because you want to, not because you feel you have to say yes. Because once you agree, you won't be able to go back to your old life. You'll be part of the clan, which means you'll have to stay here with us. You'll get a new job in the clan. You'll have to make new friends."

That could be a dealbreaker. Morven wished the queen hadn't told Sheldon about all of it, but on the other hand, he knew she'd had to. He had no idea what Sheldon would de-cide, but he wished he did.

Sheldon could tell something was wrong with Blake. He'd been quiet during the meeting with the queen, and even more so now that the meeting was over. Sheldon wanted to talk to him, but he didn't know if Blake would want that. He also didn't want to do it with an audience, which was hard, since he had no idea where to go inside the palace. He was pretty sure that if he asked Orran to give him and Blake space, Orran would leave, but that didn't sit right with him.

They were back in Orran and Blake's rooms, and the two of them belonged there. Neither of them should be asked to leave. Sheldon was the guest, and he had to find another way to make this work.

It wasn't going to be easy, with Blake avoiding looking at him.

"What's going on?" he asked softly.

He hadn't noticed yesterday when he'd arrived, but in the main room, there wasn't just a nest. There was also an area with wide cushions, which he supposed were dragons' couches. That was where he and Blake were sitting, but it was getting uncomfortable with Blake looking everywhere but at Sheldon.

Blake shrugged, still looking away. Sheldon huffed. Blake was younger than he was, but he was still an adult. If he had a problem with Sheldon, he should tell Sheldon about it.

"Come on. I know something is up, and I won't leave you alone until you tell me. I thought you'd be happy to have me with you for a few days, but if that's not the case, I can leave right away."

Blake snapped his head toward Sheldon. "You want to leave right now?"

"I don't. But if you're not going to talk to me, I don't see why I should stay."

Blake sighed and rubbed his face. "Fine. We can talk. Not here, though."

"You don't want Orran to hear us?"

"I don't want him to hear how stupid I'm being."

That didn't bode well, but what was Sheldon supposed to do? He wanted to find out what was up with his brother, and that would only happen if he did whatever Blake was asking. If Blake wanted to talk somewhere else, that was what they would do.

"I don't know the palace," Sheldon pointed out.

"Luckily, I do. I know the perfect spot."

"As long as it's not too far away. I'm not sure I'll be able to walk much."

Blake grimaced. "We can just stay here if it's better for you."

"I'm fine. Let's go."

So off they went. Sheldon was more than happy to leave Orran and Blake's rooms. He loved them for allowing him to stay with them, but he also wanted to see more of the palace. He didn't know how long he would be able to stay, and the place was huge. He wanted to explore at least a bit before going home.

If he ever actually went home.

He hadn't made his decision yet. He wanted to stay, but he also wanted to go. His brother was here, but everything else he knew was back in the city. How was he supposed to choose? It wasn't going to be easy, and he suspected that was why Blake was angry at him. It would be easier to understand if Blake actually told him about it, but when had Blake been smart about these kinds of things?

They walked slowly, and Sheldon couldn't stop looking around. They passed a few dragons, and luckily for them, none of them tried to stop them. Sheldon was pretty sure that eventually, he was going to have to face those who didn't want him here. That wasn't going to happen anytime soon, though.

Or at least, he hoped so. He didn't think he and Blake were up to dealing with unfriendly dragons right now, and he would feel better once they arrived wherever they were going. The queen had promised he was safe, but she'd hinted at him getting lost, and he wasn't stupid. He'd read between the lines, and he knew what she hadn't said. Some dragons were happy to have him and Blake there, but some weren't, and they might have something to say about it if they met Sheldon in an empty hallway.

"We're almost there," Blake said.

"Good." Sheldon was getting tired, which was ridiculous, since they hadn't walked that long. He knew it was because he was wounded, and he didn't like feeling like this. He wanted to be able to defend himself and Blake if something happened. Of course, it was more probable that Blake would be the one defending them. He'd always been the fighter between them, while Sheldon was the worrier.

They walked down a hallway and took a turn to the right. It was another hallway, but this one wasn't closed off. It opened onto the outside through wide arcs, and Sheldon couldn't help but grin at the sight.

It was beautiful. The palace was gorgeous, but so was the area around the mountain. Everywhere Sheldon looked, he could only see trees. "How can humans not know about this place?" he asked.

"I'm not sure. It's kind of obvious if you know it's there, but maybe not if you don't?"

"How could anyone miss these windows?" They didn't have glass, but it was the only thing Sheldon could call them. They were windows open to the outside world, and he took a deep breath.

The air was damp, but it wasn't raining. He wondered what this place was like in the middle of winter. Cold, probably. The dragons wouldn't have a problem with that, especially if they stuck to their dragon forms, but Blake and Sheldon would probably be freezing. Not that it would change Blake's mind.

"I wish you'd accepted the queen's offer," Blake said. He leaned against one of the windows, his focus on the outside.

"I'm thinking about it."

"Why do you have to think about it?"

"Because unlike you, I have things to go back to in the city. I have a job, and there's our family."

Blake shook his head. "I think you're using our family as

an excuse. They're not good people, Sheldon. They kicked me out because I'm gay."

And they would do the same if they found out that Sheldon liked men, too. Sheldon had never told Blake, and he wondered if now was the right moment to do that.

"Besides, can you really say no to all of this?" Blake continued.

"What do you mean?"

"The palace. The dragons. It's incredible, don't you think?"

"I never imagined something like this could be real."

"So what's the real reason you don't want to move?"

"What would I do here?"

"You could work freelance. You could even work for the dragons. I don't know. I never understood what you do with computers. I just know that as long as you have wi-fi, you can do your job anywhere you are, right?"

"I guess." But Sheldon was afraid. His life in the city wasn't much, but it was familiar and safe, while what the queen and Blake were offering wasn't.

Could he really go back to the city, though? Blake was right. Their parents weren't good people, and they wouldn't care about Sheldon if he told them about who he was. He knew Blake wouldn't have anything to say about it, though. The only reason he hadn't told his brother was that he hadn't really told anyone. He wasn't in a relationship at the moment, and he had no plans to be in one anytime soon.

An image of him and Morven twined together in the lake flashed in his mind. He almost rolled his eyes at himself, but he managed not to. Morven wasn't part of the equation. Sheldon couldn't think about him when he made the decision whether or not to move.

"I'll think about it," he said.

"I wish you could give us an answer right away." But Blake didn't look as angry anymore.

"I want to give you an answer right away, but I don't want to make a mistake. You found a family here, and I'm happy for you. I don't have anyone like Orran, though."

"You could. If Orran and I can make it work, you can make it work with a dragon, too."

Sheldon bit his lower lip. He didn't want to be rude, but he was curious. "How does it work?"

Blake frowned. "What do you mean?"

Sheldon had to look away. "You don't have to give me any details if you don't want to, but Orran isn't human, not even when he's in his human form. How does it work?"

Blake grinned. "You mean in bed?"

"Forget I asked," Sheldon said, turning around to leave.

Blake caught his arm. "Wait. I won't give you any details, but I can talk about it."

Sheldon leaned against the wall, ready to listen. He didn't have any plans to be with a dragon, but he was still curious, and if Blake was volunteering information, he wasn't going to say no.

Do we know who's behind this? the queen asked.

Morven wished he could say no, but at the same time, he was proud of the fact that he had a name. Still, it wasn't easy to tell the queen that one of her family members had his eyes on the throne and was trying to take it away from her. *I don't have any proof as of now. There are a lot of whispered conversations happening, but I heard a few of them, and I have a name. Well, I have several names.*

The queen sighed. *That means several people working against me.*

Not as many as you think, considering the clan's numbers. But at least three elders aren't happy with you, and they have the support of some of your family members. And of course, are other dragons who aren't happy, either. I don't think they're a danger, though, not unless someone tries to recruit them. If they're smart, they won't try anything.

When has anyone been smart when it comes to usurping a throne?

She had a point.

Let's start with the elders, the queen said.

Morven nodded. *The most obvious are Galatea, Harwood, and Thorley.*

Nothing we didn't expect.

Those three had been against everything and anything the queen's father suggested when he was king, too. From Morven's point of view, they should retire. There was no retiring an elder, though. That was kind of the point of having elders. They'd worked for the queen's father, and once their time to retire had come, they'd become elders, which were supposed to advise the king or queen. They didn't have a say in how the clan was led beyond that, but they had a lot of influence, and some were vocal about what they thought of the queen's reign.

What about my family? You said those elders have the support of some of them. Do I want to know who's going to stab me in the back?

I wish I could say they would never do this, but considering who it is, it's a possibility.

The queen briefly closed her eyes. *Caven.*

Morven nodded. *That's what I heard, yes.*

Caven was the queen's cousin. He'd always thought he should inherit the throne after the king died. He was a male, and like some, he thought that the queen being female meant she shouldn't lead the clan. The queen's father hadn't shared that thought, thankfully. Still, Caven had been trying to undermine the queen since she stepped into her father's shoes, and he didn't give any sign of stopping.

I always knew he would be trouble, the queen said.

So far, he hasn't done much of anything. It's definitely a possibility, though. He's been seen talking to the three elders I mentioned and to others, probably trying to convince them to support him. If he can give them proof that you're not a good leader, he might be able to sway them. If a lot of them turn against you . . .

I'll have to abdicate.

She was right. No one would force her, but could she really be a queen and lead the clan when no one wanted her to? The clan would be torn apart, and she wouldn't want that.

Someone knocked on the door. Morven frowned and stood in front of the queen, just in case. *Who is it?* he projected.

The door opened, and a guard peeked in. *Sorry to disturb you, your Majesty, but your cousin wants to talk to you.*

Which cousin? the queen asked.

Caven.

Morven looked at the queen. It couldn't be a coincidence.

She nodded and turned her attention back to the guard. *Let him in. Morven, I want you to stay with me.*

You think he's going to try something?

She shook her head. *Probably not. He's not that stupid. I could still use some support.*

I'm sure that some of your ministers would be better when it comes to that.

Maybe, but they're not here right now.

The door opened again, and Morven stood up straighter. He glared as a light blue dragon walked in. He was gorgeous, but it was only physical. Inside, Caven had always been spoiled rotten and thought that he was owed everything he wanted. The fact that he hadn't become king still angered him, which was why Morven wasn't surprised that he was actively trying to undermine the queen. They didn't have any proof of that for now, but once they did, the queen would be able to deal with it, and hopefully, Caven would stop being a problem.

I knew you were making a mistake when you allowed the first human into the clan, but now there's a second one? Caven asked.

Morven growled. *Have a bit of respect. You're in front of your queen.*

Caven glared at Morven. He bowed his head just the tiniest bit, then faced the queen again. *How can you do this? Humans want to kill us. You can't allow them to stay.*

Well, I already have, and I don't see how it's your problem. I wouldn't have done it if I'd thought they were dangerous to us.

How can you say they're not? They're a stain on the earth. You can't trust any of them, and if you allow those two to stay here, they're eventually going to hurt us. You saw what happened to your son. How can you trust humans?

Morven had always suspected Caven to be behind the kidnapping of Blue's egg. He didn't have any proof. Caven might be spoiled and arrogant, but he was also smart, unfortunately.

The queen didn't get up, but she stared at Caven until he took a step back. Once he had, she nodded. *I listened to your doubts, and I'll take them into consideration. But I've already made my decision. If the humans want to stay with us, they're allowed to.*

You can't trust them with your son.

Why not? You're right. Humans kidnapped Blue. It wasn't a human who let them into the palace, though. That was a dragon.

And you caught him.

They had. The dragon hadn't had a reason to allow humans into the palace, though, or to have them kidnap Blue. He'd taken the fall for whoever had given him orders, and so far, he hadn't told them as much as a name. Morven wasn't giving up, but he had to focus on other things.

We did, but that points to the fact that humans aren't the only people who are dangerous to us. Dragons are dangerous to each other, too, and I don't think that allowing two humans to stay with us is going to change that. Any of us could eat them with one bite. What can they do? There are only two of them, and humans have always been stronger against us in groups.

You're going to regret this, Caven snapped.

Morven stepped in front of the queen again. *Are you threatening the queen?*

Caven looked like he wanted to say yes, but he took another step back. *I wouldn't dare.*

Sure he wouldn't. Morven continued to glare at him. He wanted Caven to know that whatever he thought, Morven wouldn't allow him to hurt the queen.

Mark my words, Caven continued. *You're going to regret this. The humans are going to break your trust, and then you'll have nothing to show for it. Do you really think the clan should have a leader who does this kind of thing? We won't go along with it.*

As long as I'm the queen, you have to, the queen said.

Maybe you won't be the queen for long.

Morven wanted to knock Caven on his ass, but he knew better. Even though he hated the dragon, Caven was still part of the royal family. If he were to be touched, it had to come from a royal order, given by the queen. If Morven as much as ruffled his ego, he would complain to the queen and make sure Morven paid for it. And if Morven wasn't there anymore, the queen would be more vulnerable.

Thankfully, Caven turned around and left. Morven couldn't help but wonder why he'd revealed his hand this way. They'd known he wasn't happy with the queen's decisions, but so far, he hadn't been vocal about it.

It isn't over, the queen said.

Morven had to agree. *I'll keep you safe.*

I know you will. I wonder if it'll be enough.

Morven wondered the same thing.

CHAPTER SIX

The palace was even bigger than Sheldon had expected. He'd seen how big the mountain was, but he hadn't thought the dragons had dug out its entirety. He suspected that wasn't the case, either. Still, the space they *had* dug was huge, and he was already getting tired.

He and Blake had been exploring for a few days. There was so much to see and so little time for Sheldon to do it. He hadn't given the queen an answer yet, but he knew he would have to soon.

"I have to go to work," Blake said.

Sheldon hadn't met Blue yet, and he wasn't sure he would be allowed to. He was curious, though. Blake had sacrificed his old life for the baby dragon, but he had found a different one thanks to him. "I can get back to your rooms on my own."

"How about you come with me?"

"As long as it's allowed. The queen hasn't said anything about me meeting her son. I don't want to do something I shouldn't be doing."

"She would have told me if you weren't allowed to. Don't worry. Besides, I *want* you to meet Blue. He's adorable."

Sheldon couldn't help but smile. Blake had been talking about Blue almost as much as he talked about Orran, which was already a lot. It was obvious his life here revolved around the two, and Sheldon was happy for him. He'd been alone for so long, with no one to care for him or to care about. Now that had changed, and Blake was glowing. He'd truly found his path with the dragons, and Sheldon knew he would never leave them. This was Blake's place now, no matter how hard it was.

Sheldon wasn't sure it could be his place, too.

"All right. Introduce me to him, then."

Blake beamed and headed down the hallway. Sheldon followed, glad that he was healing. He wouldn't have been able to keep up with his brother otherwise, even though he was pushing himself. Blake was happier than he'd ever been, which translated into him having a lot of energy. Sheldon hadn't said anything because he didn't want his brother to change the way he was behaving, but it was getting tiring. His ribs were still healing, and it would take a while to get to the point where they didn't hurt. Sheldon supposed he should be lucky that at least the bruises and the swelling were fading.

"What do you teach him?" Sheldon asked.

"Whatever I feel like for now. He's still very young, which is why I thought it didn't make sense for him to have a tutor already. It's tradition, though. I have to say that Orran and I are more like babysitters for now, but that's going to change in time. I tell Blue about the human world, how it works, how beautiful it can be. I told him about you, too."

"Why?"

"Because I wanted to. You're my family, Sheldon."

Sheldon looked away. Blake wasn't saying those words lightly. Sheldon was the only family he had left, while Sheldon still had their parents. Sometimes, he wondered what his life would be like without them.

He was living that life right now. He didn't have his phone with him, so his parents couldn't try calling him and demanding things from him. He hadn't called the plumber, which meant that the kitchen sink was still leaking. His mother wouldn't care, but his father would be angry at him for not solving the problem.

That was what Sheldon was to them. He was a problem

solver and not much else. He often wondered why they'd had children if they didn't seem to be able to care for them. They hadn't had a problem kicking Blake out when he'd come out to them, which pointed to the fact that they'd never actually loved him. Maybe they didn't love Sheldon, either. He would be out the door quickly if he came out to them.

He cleared his throat. So far, he hadn't found the perfect moment to tell Blake about his sexuality. He wanted to, but he was afraid Blake would use it as leverage to convince him to stay.

And Sheldon wanted to stay. How could he not? Blake was offering him so much. But it was also terrifying. Sheldon didn't know a lot about the clan and how tense things were, but not everyone liked the fact that he and Blake were there. It was scary, because a dragon could hurt him so easily.

"We're here," Blake declared.

Sheldon blinked. They were standing in front of a door. It was as big as all of the other doors in the palace, but it wasn't ornate.

Blake pushed it open and walked in. Something screeched, and Blake stumbled when a blue ball hit his chest. He laughed, and Sheldon realized it was a baby dragon.

The baby scrambled up Blake's chest and rubbed his face against Blake's. Blake's expression softened, and he stroked the baby's back. Then, he turned toward Sheldon. "Sheldon, this is Blue. Blue, this is my brother, Sheldon."

The baby peeked at Sheldon. When he saw Sheldon looking at him, he buried his face against Blake's neck.

Sheldon couldn't help but smile. Blue truly was adorable, and he could see why Blake wanted to stay here and protect the baby.

"Why don't you sit down?" Blake asked Sheldon. "It's going to take him a bit to get used to you. I'm the only human he knows, and the other ones he met weren't exactly friendly.

Don't get offended if he doesn't want to come to you."

"I won't. I never expected him to." Sheldon sat on a bench under the window and continued observing Blue and his brother.

It was incredible. Blue clearly loved Blake, and Blake loved Blue. They were relaxed with each other, and it made Sheldon's heart ache. It had been a long time since he'd last seen his brother like this, and he didn't want to hurt Blake. He wanted to stay here with him, but he wasn't sure he could.

He had to think things through. He'd been thinking about it since the beginning, of course, but it wasn't enough. His brother was always there, trying to convince him. He was never pushy, but it was hard to say no to him when he was right there in front of Sheldon. Sheldon needed some time alone, even though Blake wasn't going to be happy about it.

"I think I'm going to go back to the rooms," Sheldon said as he got to his feet.

Blake frowned and turned to him. "Is something wrong?"

"I'm just tired. Still healing, you know?"

"I'll walk you there."

"You don't have to. I remember the way. It's not far."

"It's not, but you could get lost easily. I did a few times when I first arrived."

"I'll be fine. You have work to do, and you can't spend your time babysitting me." Sheldon cautiously reached out to Blue. He let the dragon examine his fingers, hoping he wasn't about to bite them. To his surprise, Blue made a purring sound and stroked his cheek against them.

Sheldon smiled and stroked back. "It was a pleasure to meet you," he murmured. Then, he took a step back. "I'll be in the guest room. Don't worry about me. I think I'm going to take a nap." And hopefully, make a decision.

Blake didn't look convinced, but he didn't have a choice. He couldn't leave Blue, not when he was supposed to teach him his lessons. Sheldon snuck out, taking a deep breath as soon as the door closed behind him. He didn't have a lot of time, and by the end of it, he needed to have made his decision.

Of course, he got lost.

He hadn't lied when he'd told Blake he thought he could find his way, but he'd been wrong. He took a few wrong turns until he couldn't recognize the area of the palace he was in. He looked around, biting his lip. He was alone, so there was no one he could ask for directions. He was pretty sure he shouldn't ask anyone anyway. How was he supposed to know which dragon was friendly and which wasn't?

He turned to the left, swearing when he saw it was a dead end. He touched the wall in front of him, feeling the still rough stone under his fingertips. The dragons were expanding the palace, and they weren't done with this part yet.

He turned around to head back and froze. A dragon was standing in the middle of the hallway, glaring at him. It was bright yellow, which didn't go with the glare.

Sheldon raised his hand and waved. "Hi. I'm sorry if I came to an area I shouldn't be in, but I got lost. I'll go as soon as you point out the right way."

The dragon continued staring. Sheldon was pretty sure he wasn't going to get directions, and he was stunned when the dragon shifted. It seemed like every single dragon Sheldon had seen in their human form was gorgeous, and this one wasn't an exception. His characteristics were harder than Sheldon liked, but it gave him a certain charm.

The glare didn't.

"This isn't your place," the dragon said.

Sheldon had already guessed that was what he was going for. "As I said, I'm trying to go back to my room."

"You need to leave the mountain. Go back to your city."

So this was one of the dragons who weren't happy with

Sheldon and Blake's presence at the palace. "I just might."

"Something bad will happen to you if you don't."

Sheldon was terrified, but he wasn't going to allow anyone to push him into deciding between staying or leaving. "Is that a threat?"

The dragon smiled. "It's more than a threat. It's a promise."

Sheldon took a step back, but it was too late. The dragon backhanded him, making him fly. When his back hit the wall, it felt like his ribs broke a second time. Sheldon was out of breath, but he tried to get to his feet. He knew he wouldn't be able to when the dragon stalked toward him. He'd shifted back, and Sheldon was pretty sure he was about to be eaten.

A loud roar made him jump. It looked like the dragon was going to have help.

Morven was livid. Sheldon was lucky he'd been passing through this area. He wanted to tear this dragon apart to make sure he would never hurt anyone else.

How dare you hurt the queen's guest? he projected.

He's a human. He deserves to die for what he did to dragons.

Sheldon has never done anything to dragons. Do you really want to kill an innocent?

The dragon looked like he was going to say yes, and Morven roared at him again.

The dragon took a step back, away from Sheldon.

There will be consequences to this. The queen won't allow you to just go back to your life after you hit Sheldon. You should have thought better about what you were doing.

It's not right. He shouldn't be there, and I'm not the only one who thinks that way. You might have won this fight, but we'll win the war.

Morven arched a brow. *I wasn't aware there was a war.*

The dragon grinned. *You're more stupid than I thought, then.*

Morven was trying to remember where he'd seen the

dragon. He was sure it wasn't the first time they met, which meant this dragon was either a guard—but Morven didn't recognize him as one—or someone he could have seen around the queen. Morven didn't have time to socialize outside his little group, so it couldn't be that.

He was pretty sure this dragon had something to do with Caven. He was going to have to look into it. He wanted to fight, but he was on his own, and Sheldon was hurt. He was still crumbled against the wall, holding his ribs, and Morven had to resist the urge to run to him.

He waited until the dragon left. He would find him again, and when he did, he would make sure the dragon paid for what he'd done. As soon as the dragon turned the corner, Morven shifted and rushed to Sheldon. "What happened?"

Sheldon groaned. "I had a hard encounter with the wall."

"You're not funny." Morven gently took Sheldon's hands and hauled him to his feet. "You're in pain."

"You're observant," Sheldon answered.

He was irritating and frustrating, but Morven was happy he felt well enough to joke. "Let's get you back to your room. I should probably call a healer."

"Maybe it's not a bad idea."

Morven reached down and lifted Sheldon as gently as he could. Sheldon still squeaked and wrapped his arms around Morven's neck.

"What are you doing?" he asked.

"Taking you back to your room."

"I can walk."

"I don't want you to have to. You're in pain. You were just attacked, and you're probably terrified. Allow me to do this for you." Morven desperately wanted Sheldon to see that not all dragons were like the one who had attacked him. He didn't want Sheldon to run away because he was afraid of what was going to happen to him if he stayed.

He wanted Sheldon to stay.

He walked as fast as he could without hurting Sheldon even more, but he was aware of the fact that every step jostled Sheldon's ribs. Sheldon didn't say anything about it. Instead, he buried his face against Morven's neck. He wasn't going to protest, even though he was in pain, and once again, Morven wanted to get his hands on that dragon and strangle him.

He was relieved when he reached the door to Orran's rooms. He quickly knocked before opening, noticed no one was there, then turned his attention to Sheldon. "Where are you sleeping?"

Sheldon gestured to the door at the back of the room. "Guest room."

Morven nodded and headed that way. This room was smaller, although still big enough to host a dragon. He gently lowered Sheldon to the nest, not missing the way Sheldon winced every time he moved. As soon as Sheldon was down, Morven got to his feet. "I'm going to find a healer."

To his surprise, Sheldon grabbed his hand and pulled him back. "Not yet. Please. I know I need to see a healer, but I don't want to be alone right now."

Sheldon was obviously terrified. Anyone would be after that kind of encounter with a dragon. He was lucky he was alive and in one piece. If Morven hadn't passed by, he probably wouldn't be.

Morven tightened his free hand until his claws dug small wounds into his palms. "I'm sorry you had to go through that."

"It wasn't your fault. I knew some people weren't happy about my presence here, but I never thought I'd be attacked."

"You shouldn't have been. I'll make sure he pays for what he did to you."

Sheldon shook his head. "I'm fine. I promise."

"Will you allow me to check your ribs? I'm not a healer, but

I have some experience when it comes to this kind of thing." It was necessary when one was a guard.

Sheldon looked away, his cheeks pink. "If you absolutely have to. There's no need, though. I already feel better."

"That doesn't mean you're not hurt."

Sheldon nodded tightly, and Morven reached for the bottom of his borrowed shirt. He lifted it, wincing at the sight of the bruises along Sheldon's chest. He gently touched the skin, and even though Sheldon was clearly in pain, he didn't try to move away.

"I don't think anything else broke." Morven turned his attention to Sheldon's face. "You're going to have a new bruise on your face, though."

Sheldon rolled his eyes. "Of course I will."

"I'll kill him for what he did to you."

"Don't even talk that way. I don't want you to get hurt because of this. I'm fine."

He was, mostly. Morven should be backing down, especially since Sheldon didn't want him to do any of this. Why wasn't he?

Because he cared about Sheldon. He didn't know when it had happened, but the human had worked his way under his skin. Now, Sheldon was anchored there, and Morven was angry that he hadn't been able to protect the man he cared so much about.

He was terrified of losing Sheldon. He couldn't ignore that, not after what happened. It had been almost easy to push his growing feelings for Sheldon into a small box at the back of his mind until now, but the box had burst open, and Morven couldn't ignore it anymore.

He was afraid of losing Sheldon. He didn't want Sheldon to go back to the human world. He wanted Sheldon to stay, and he wanted what Orran and Blake had.

Morven sucked in a breath. "I was afraid for you."

Sheldon smiled at him. "I was afraid for myself. I'm fine, though. I promise."

Morven nodded and caught one of Sheldon's hands. "Thank the sky for that. I don't want to lose you."

Sheldon frowned. "What do you mean?"

Morven cupped one of Sheldon's cheeks with his free hand and lowered himself until his face was hovering just above Sheldon's. Sheldon's eyes were wide, but he didn't try to push Morven away when he kissed him.

This wasn't supposed to happen. Sheldon wasn't supposed to fall half in love with a dragon and want to stay, especially not after what had just happened to him.

Right now, though, he could think of nothing that wasn't the dragon on top of him.

Morven kissed like a dream. Sheldon had expected it to be strange, but it wasn't. The kiss was passionate and told him how Morven felt about him, and while he knew that the fear of losing him had played an important role in this situation, he couldn't find it in himself to be sorry about it.

He'd been terrified, but it had led to this.

He hooked his hands around Morven's neck and hung on for dear life. He'd known Morven was passionate, and not merely for his work. Just from the kiss, Sheldon could tell he would be a good lover. He was slow, coaxing Sheldon's tongue out of his mouth, giving him time to move away and to get used to the kiss. Sheldon almost wanted Morven to throw caution to the wind and kiss him into next week.

He pushed up, needing more. He buried his fingers into Morven's green hair, gently pulling, smiling when Morven groaned.

Morven let go of Sheldon's hand and wrapped himself around Sheldon more effectively. His fingers slipped under

Sheldon's t-shirt, stroking his skin.

Sheldon couldn't stop himself from doing the same. The fact that Morven was naked seemed like a good thing right now, because it gave Sheldon easy access. He ran his fingertips down Morven's sides and around his back. Morven was different, yet he was also the same as Sheldon. He was solid under Sheldon's touch, safe, and Sheldon never wanted this to end.

Something hard poked his groin, and his eyes widened. Even though he hadn't wanted to stare, he'd gotten his fair share of peeks at the dragons in their human form since he'd arrived at the palace. He also knew what Blake had told him, so he was aware of the fact that dragons had a pouch. It was where the male dragons' sexual organs were hidden until they were aroused. When that happened, their cocks slid out.

Which was exactly what was going on between Sheldon and Morven's bodies.

It gave Sheldon a jolt, and it reminded him of everything that had just happened. He wanted to continue kissing Morven and see where this could go, but at the same time, he needed space to breathe.

He tore his lips from Morven's, sucking in a deep breath.

"Sheldon?" Morven asked. His voice was rough.

It made Sheldon want to kiss him again. "I'm sorry. It's my ribs." It wasn't a lie. Now that they'd stopped kissing, Sheldon could feel his ribs pulsing. He desperately wanted a painkiller.

Morven scrambled off Sheldon's body. "I'm sorry."

Sheldon shook his head and reached for Morven. He'd wanted to slow things down, but he didn't want Morven to leave. "It's fine."

"It's not fine." Morven sat next to Sheldon, close enough to touch him.

Sheldon wished he was even closer, but he didn't ask for

it. "I'm sure I'll be okay."

"What happened?"

Sheldon sighed and stared at the ceiling. "I went to visit Blue with Blake. When I told Blake I wanted to come back here, he offered to walk me here, but I refused. He had to work, and I thought I could find my way. Instead, I got lost. I ended up in that dead-end, and when I turned around, that other dragon was there."

"What did he do to you?"

"Apart from hitting me? Not much. He threatened me, told me this wasn't my place and that I was going to regret being here." Or something like that. Sheldon didn't remember the exact words, and if he had his way, he would never think about them again.

He was terrified. He'd known some people weren't happy with his presence at the palace, but he hadn't realized just how much he was hated. How was he supposed to agree to stay when this kind of thing could happen? He'd been lucky this time because Morven had been passing by, but what about next time? Sheldon couldn't live his entire life in fear, just like he couldn't ask for a bodyguard who would protect him every time he took a step in the palace.

"You weren't kidding when you said that some people weren't happy about Blake and me," he murmured.

"I wanted you to know what you were going against if you decided to stay."

"I almost did."

"You changed your mind?"

Sheldon shrugged. "I don't know. It would be safer for me to go back to the city." But then, he would be alone again. He wouldn't have Blake, and he wouldn't have Morven. His parents couldn't compare.

"It would," Morven confirmed.

"But I would be leaving my brother here alone, and I don't

want to do that, either. I allowed our parents to push us apart, and it was a mistake. Now that I have him back, I don't want to lose him a second time."

"I don't think you would."

"What do *you* want? Do you want me to stay?"

Morven stared down at Sheldon while Sheldon held his breath. "I can't tell you what to do or not to do," Morven finally said.

"That's not what I asked."

"My answer will influence you, though, won't it? It's why you're asking. You have a difficult decision to make, and you're the only one who can make it. You only have to think about yourself when it comes to it. Ignore Blake and me. Think about what *you* want to do and what would be better for you."

The problem with that was that it was impossible. Sheldon couldn't just think about himself. He wasn't an island. There were people in his life, people he cared about, and people he didn't want to hurt. Leaving them behind would hurt them, no matter how cagey Morven was being right now.

But staying would hurt Sheldon. He was pretty sure that if he had another encounter like the one he'd just had, he wouldn't walk out of it alive.

Morven wanted to reach for Sheldon and promise everything would be okay. He wanted to ask Sheldon to stay and see if whatever was between them could mean something. He also wanted to strangle the dragon who'd threatened and attacked Sheldon, but none of those things would be happening.

Sheldon needed time and to be able to make this decision on his own. It would flip his life upside down, and it wasn't something to take lightly.

"I want to stay," Sheldon said.

Morven made sure to avoid getting closer. "But?" He didn't want to influence Sheldon or for Sheldon to make the wrong choice for himself.

"But I'm scared. That dragon wasn't playing around. If you hadn't happened to be there . . ."

Sheldon would probably be dead. They both knew it, even though they didn't say it out loud. "I have to alert the queen. She needs to know what happened."

Sheldon tried to sit up and winced. He held his ribs and looked at Morven with wide eyes. "You're leaving?"

Morven should. Sheldon needed time and space. He'd had an eventful day, to say the least. Morven could see that being alone scared him, though. "I can stay if you want me to."

He'd do pretty much anything for Sheldon, and he didn't understand it. They still barely knew each other. When had Sheldon become so important to him? When had he gone from being a mildly interesting human to someone to protect and cherish?

"Please. I know it's probably not the best thing right now and that you have work to do, but I'd rather not be alone."

"Do you want me to call your brother?"

Sheldon hesitated. "He'd freak out, and I don't want that to happen. If it's not a problem for you, I'd rather stay with you. Let him do his job and be with Blue. He'll find out about this soon enough anyway."

Sheldon wasn't wrong. Blake had other things to focus on, and while he should know what had happened to his brother, Sheldon was okay. He was safe, and there would be time to tell Blake about this. Sheldon was the one making decisions. If he didn't want Blake to know right now, that was what Morven would do.

"I'll shift. Stay where you are."

Morven extracted himself from the nest, and he wasn't surprised when Sheldon followed his movements with his gaze.

"Are you going to the other room?" he asked.

He looked like he would freak out if Morven did. "I can stay in the room, but I don't want to shift so close to you. I don't want to risk hurting you, even by accident."

Sheldon bit his lower lip and looked away. "After you're done giving the queen your message, can you come back here?"

"Of course."

"I mean in your dragon form. I know it's weird, but—"

"It's not." If anything, Sheldon's request made Morven's heart beat faster.

Clearly, Sheldon wasn't just fascinated by dragons the way most humans were. They would be more than happy to watch Morven at a distance, but they would be terrified of him. Sheldon was probably scared, too, especially after what had just happened to him, but he knew Morven would protect him, whether he was in his dragon form or not. The fact that he wanted to be so close to a dragon after one had just attacked him made Morven hope. Yes, Sheldon was scared, but he wasn't letting fear rule him.

Sheldon nodded and relaxed into the nest. Morven wanted to stay, but he had work to do. He got to his feet and stepped out of the nest, shifting right away. He didn't have to be careful, even though this was Sheldon's room. He was still at the palace, and it was made for dragons.

Your Majesty? Morven projected.

It took her a moment to answer, but Morven had expected that. As he waited, he twisted his tail so that it curled into the nest around Sheldon. Sheldon jerked, but he didn't move away. Instead, he snuggled closer, sighing in what sounded like relief.

Morven? the queen finally answered.

Morven had to gather his thoughts. *Sheldon was attacked.*

How is he? Does he need a healer?

I would like a healer to look at him, but he seems okay. He's moving all right, and he's talking.

Where is he? What happened? She paused. *Are you sure he's okay?*

I checked his wounds, and they seem to be only a little worse. He was lucky I was passing by. He was in an area of the palace still under construction. He got lost.

Who attacked him?

I don't know his name. I wanted to arrest him and confront him, but I thought it would be better for me to focus on Sheldon. I think I can find the attacker easily enough, though. I'm pretty sure I've seen him in the past, and that means he's either a guard, and I'm sure he's not, or someone else I met for work.

You think he's close to me.

If not to you, to someone close to you. And they both knew who that dragon would be.

We can't accuse Caven, not when we're not sure he has anything to do with this.

I'm not accusing him. We both know it's probable that he was involved, though. What would be the odds that he wasn't? But Morven knew that even if he found out that the yellow dragon was Caven's best friend, he couldn't accuse Caven without proof. The dragon was the queen's cousin, which gave him a certain immunity. As soon as Morven had evidence, though, he would bring it to the queen, and she would take care of Caven.

There was no doubt in Morven's mind that Caven had something to do with the attack. He didn't want Blake and Sheldon at the palace or the queen on the throne. He would do anything to make both those things happen, including killing the humans.

Morven wouldn't allow him to do that.

Are you with Sheldon? the queen asked.

I am. He didn't want me to contact his brother, but I think I'm going to have to.

Contact Orran. He can break the news to Blake. And take the rest of the day off and be with Sheldon.

Morven frowned. *I need to protect you.*

You need to protect the throne. If that means staying with Sheldon for the rest of the day, then so be it. He's more important.

I begged to differ, Your Majesty.

She chuckled. *I know you trust the guards you put with me. They'll protect me. Besides, I doubt anyone is going to try to attack me, especially not after the failed attack against Sheldon. But if something happened to him or his brother, it would reflect on my authority. Stay with him. Protect him and make sure he's okay.* She hesitated. *See if you can convince him to stay.*

Why do you want him to stay so much? I can understand Blake, since he saved your son, but Sheldon?

I truly believe in dragons and humans living together. This is the first step to making that happen, but if Sheldon leaves, it won't. I don't want the dragons to have to be isolated. I realize it will take much more than two humans to change things, but it's the first step. Even if it takes hundreds of years, I want to see this through.

I'll stay with him. Even though Morven should go back to work, he was selfish. The queen had ordered him to stay with Sheldon, and he would do just that.

Good.

Right after he was done talking to the queen, Morven contacted Orran. His friend was understandably alarmed, and he promised to tell Blake but also to make sure he didn't barge into Sheldon's room to make sure he was okay. Sheldon needed space, and Morven would make sure he got it.

Once he was done talking to everyone he had to talk to, he turned toward the nest. Sheldon's eyes were closed, but Morven didn't think he was sleeping. His breath wasn't regular enough.

Since Sheldon had asked him to get into the nest without shifting, Morven obeyed. Hopefully, it would be the first time they did this, but not the last.

He climbed in, careful not to jostle Sheldon. Sheldon

opened his eyes, but he didn't move. He allowed Morven to curl himself around him, and even though his cheeks were pink by the time Morven had his head pressing against Sheldon's, he relaxed.

It was strange, but it felt good. Sheldon obviously trusted Morven, and it made Morven both smug and happy. He watched as Sheldon relaxed and his eyes fluttered close, and finally, his breathing became more regular. He was asleep, which meant that he truly trusted Morven.

Morven sighed. He wanted to be worth Sheldon's thrust, which meant that he was going to have to find the dragon who had attacked him and make sure it didn't happen again.

CHAPTER SEVEN

Sheldon was afraid of walking around the palace on his own. No one would blame him for it. Morven certainly didn't. Still, Sheldon would have felt safer if Morven was with him.

Morven had work to do, though. He'd spent the entire day of the attack with Sheldon, but he'd had to leave eventually. That had been a few days ago, and Sheldon had barely seen him since then. He was surprised to realize that he missed Morven, but maybe he shouldn't be. He'd already felt drawn to him before, and the attack had pushed them even closer.

His cheeks heated. They'd kissed — and what a kiss it had been. Sheldon wanted to do it again, but he knew better than to look for Morven for that purpose. Not that Morven would berate him for it, but he was protecting the queen and looking for the dragon who had attacked Sheldon. He had to focus on that, not on kissing Sheldon.

A knock on his bedroom door made Sheldon jump. He eyed it, wondering who was there, even though he knew it could only be one of two people. "Yes?" he called out.

The door opened, and Blake peeked in. He looked straight at the nest, already knowing that was where Sheldon would be. "You're still in bed."

"Did you need anything? I'm healing, and I need rest."

Blake stepped into the room. "You need fresh air."

Sheldon cringed. The last time he'd had fresh air had almost been the *last* time for him. "The healer said I had to rest."

"I don't think he meant that you had to stay in bed for an

entire week."

Sheldon glared. "It hasn't been an entire week. Just a few days."

Blake sighed. "You're right. It hasn't been that long, and I should stop pushing. I hate seeing you like this, though."

Sheldon felt guilty. He knew what his brother meant, even though Blake didn't say the words. He was terrified that Sheldon would decide to go home to the city and never come back after what had happened.

Sheldon almost had. After Morven had left him the day of the attack, he'd panicked. He'd felt safe with Morven, but once he was gone, he didn't anymore. That had passed, though. He realized that Morven wasn't the only dragon he could trust. There were others, and Sheldon had to make sure to stick with those instead of exploring the palace on his own.

That was more than fine with him.

But he still hadn't made his decision. He wanted to stay, but he was terrified at the thought that something would happen to him. He couldn't even leave his bedroom without feeling afraid. How could he move here?

"I'd like to go for a walk," Blake said.

"I don't know if it's a good idea."

"I want to show you that most dragons are welcoming. They might not know what to make of us, but they won't hurt us. The dragon who attacked you was an exception, and you need to understand that."

"I do understand it."

"I don't think you do, not really. You're afraid. It's understandable, and I won't push if you say no, but I want you to give the palace and the dragons a chance. Don't put all of them in the same box when only one of them wanted to hurt you."

"I haven't." But Sheldon was afraid to face other dragons. There was no denying that, and he would have to get over it if he was going to stay. Besides, Blake wasn't wrong. He probably could do with some fresh air and a bit of exercise.

He pushed himself to his feet. "Fine. I'll come with you."

Blake's expression told Sheldon how happy he was with that decision. "Great. I promise you'll be safe. I'll make sure you are."

Sheldon laughed. "You're human." But at least if they were attacked again, Sheldon wouldn't be alone. "We'll stick to well-frequented hallways, right?"

"Of course. I promised Orran I would be careful, and I will be. I won't let the dragons keep us in these rooms, though. We have as much right to be here as any of them."

Sheldon wasn't too sure about that. Even though the queen had allowed them to stay, they weren't dragons. They didn't belong here.

Or maybe they did.

He couldn't deny Blake looked like *he* belonged as they walked down the palace hallways. He knew where he was going, and even though no dragon they passed by stopped to talk to them, Blake smiled and nodded at them. It was apparent he recognized at least some of them, and it made Sheldon see that he truly was a part of the clan now. It didn't matter to Blake that some dragons didn't want him to be. He wasn't going anywhere.

Was Sheldon, though? It was the question Sheldon hadn't been able to answer yet, and he needed to. The queen hadn't demanded an answer yet, thankfully. After the attack, she'd left him alone, but that wouldn't last forever. He had to tell her what he'd decided, but the problem was that he hadn't decided anything.

"What's going on between you and Morven?" Blake asked suddenly.

Sheldon blinked. "What?"

Blake was smiling, so Sheldon knew he wouldn't take it

badly if he explained. He wasn't quite sure what had happened with Morven, though.

"He's been very protective of you. Also, there's the fact that when I came back to our rooms after the attack, he was curled around you. He was protecting you, but it was more than that. He was making sure you were comfortable, and you two were snuggling."

Sheldon's cheeks felt like they were on fire. "We weren't snuggling."

"I don't know what else you would call that." Blake paused. "You don't have to tell me if you don't want to, but I hope you know you can trust me. We haven't had the best relationship after our parents kicked me out, but I love you. You're my brother. You're the most important person after Orran."

Sheldon rolled his eyes. "Of course I come after your boyfriend."

Blake laughed and knocked their shoulders together. Thankfully, Sheldon's ribs barely hurt. He would have to thank the healer for the painkillers he was still taking.

"You're my family," Blake said. "You'll always be important to me."

Sheldon swallowed. "I'm not sure what's happening with Morven. I just know that after he found me, he took me back to my room, and we kissed. I'm pretty sure we would have done more if I hadn't been hurt and freaking out."

"Were you freaking out because of the attack or because of what was happening between you and Morven?"

Sheldon swallowed. "Both? It wasn't the same kind of freaking out, though. I don't know what to do with Morven. He's human, yet he's not. When it became obvious, I had to slow things down."

Blake nodded. "It's understandable, and I know Morven wouldn't care if you told him about it. I'm pretty sure he's as freaked out about your body as you are about his. Remember that you might not know how to deal with a dragon's body, but the same goes for him. He's never seen a human's naked body."

Sheldon wasn't entirely reassured by that. "Can you help me?"

"What kind of help do you want from me?"

"What am I supposed to do? To touch? Or *not* to touch?" Sheldon wanted anything that happened between him and Morven to be as good for Morven as it would be for him.

He frowned as he realized something. "You don't sound surprised about the fact that Morven is male, yet I'm interested in him."

Blake's smile was soft. "I'm not. I always suspected."

"You never told me."

"Because it's not something I could push you into admitting. I came out on my own terms, and after that disaster, I could understand why you didn't want to."

"You're not angry?"

"No. A bit disappointed, but I know we weren't as close as we should have been. I want that to change, though." Blake hesitated. "But if anything could happen with Morven, you probably should put a stop to it if you're planning on leaving. I haven't known him long, and I can see that you're important to him. He would be hurt if you got with him and left, and I'm pretty sure you would be, too. I won't lecture you, but please. Think about both your hearts."

Blake was right. Sheldon couldn't allow anything to happen with Morven if he decided not to stay. It would hurt too much to leave Morven behind when he went home.

But would he?

Morven had found him. He'd found the dragon who'd

attacked Sheldon, and now that dragon was going to pay. As much as Morven wanted to do that himself, he knew he couldn't, which was why he was standing next to the queen's throne as they both waited for the guards to walk the dragon inside.

Morven was right. Janek was close to Caven. They'd grown up together, and from what Morven knew, Janek would do pretty much anything for Caven. He was devoted, but unfortunately for him, it was to the wrong person.

A knock on the doors made Morven straighten. The doors opened, and two guards and Janek stepped in. Janek looked like he wanted to tear someone's head off, and he probably did.

He also wasn't alone.

Morven should have expected Caven to come along, but he hadn't. He'd thought Caven would try to play innocent and like he hadn't known anything about the situation, but instead, he stood next to Janek, looking defiant.

What's the meaning of this? Caven asked.

Morven growled. He couldn't help it, even though he knew it was unprofessional. Luckily for him, Caven barely even looked at him. His attention was on the queen.

Caven, she said, inclining her head at her cousin and not pointing out that he hadn't done the same, even though it was simple courtesy. *I didn't expect you to be here.*

You sent your guards to seize one of my best friends. What did you expect I would do? Why are we here?

Your friend attacked one of my guests.

You mean one of the humans.

You were aware of it?

Caven seemed to realize he'd said the wrong thing. *No, but they're your only guests. Is that what happened?*

The queen turned her attention back to Janek. *What do you have to say for yourself?*

Those humans shouldn't be here, Janek growled.

The guards framing him had been tense before, but they went ramrod straight now. They were ready to do anything to protect their queen, which was why Morven had chosen them to pick up Janek.

Maybe, but I am the queen. I'm the one who makes these decisions, not you. You knew the human was my guest, yet you attacked him. You probably would have done a lot worse if Morven hadn't happened to pass by.

You can't know what I would have done.

Not for sure, no. But attacking a guest of the queen is enough. You knew you were going against my orders when you attacked Sheldon, and you could have seriously hurt him. She paused.

Morven felt like everyone in the room was waiting for her to continue.

I condemn you to exile.

Morven sucked in a breath. It was harsher than he'd expected, yet the proper punishment. She would have demanded death if Sheldon had been more seriously hurt — or worse — but as it was, it was a fitting punishment.

Caven didn't share that opinion. *You can't exile Janek for this!*

I can exile him for whatever I see fit. The queen sat up straighter. *Him and anyone else. He knew what he was doing, and he has to pay for it. Sheldon is my guest. Blake is a clan member. They should be respected and treated as such.*

Only because you decided they should be. Not everyone agrees with that decision, and you should be careful.

The queen arched a brow. *Is that a threat?*

It's a promise. You made a mistake when you allowed one human to move into the palace, and you made it worse with the second one. People won't let you continue down this path without doing anything.

You mean you won't let me?

Caven looked lost for a moment. *No. I had nothing to do with this. I wouldn't disrespect you or your guests this way.*

That was a lie, and Morven was sure everyone in the room knew it. No one pointed it out, though. They couldn't afford to open that can of worms, not when they didn't know how to deal with it yet.

The queen looked at Morven, who turned his attention to the guards standing next to Janek. He nodded at them, and they sprang into action. They moved until Janek was forced to step back. He looked ready to kill, but thankfully, he didn't try anything. He allowed the guards to guide him out of the room.

When the doors closed behind them, the silence was heavy. Morven suspected Caven wasn't done yet, so he wasn't surprised when the queen's cousin glared at her.

You'll regret this, he told her.

I'm sure I'll regret a lot of things, but not protecting the life of an innocent human being won't be one of them.

We'll see.

Caven turned around without bowing and stomped his way out of the throne room. The guards standing by the doors closed them once he'd left, and Morven turned to the queen.

He's going to use this against you.

She nodded. She'd looked regal before, and she still did, but she also was visibly tired. *He will. We already knew that, though. I don't think there's anything we can do about it. We'll have to wait it out and see what he's planning. Unless you have proof that he was involved?*

I didn't learn anything that would point that way, Morven had to admit. They both knew Caven was at the root of this, but until they could prove it, they couldn't do anything. *You have supporters, though. Most of the elders and clan members are either neutral or happy to have Blake and Sheldon with us.*

For now. I have no doubt that Caven will try to change that.

He can't change the mind of the entire clan. It was easy to focus on the negatives in this situation, but there were positives. Some elders remembered what life with humans was like.

They were delighted that the queen wanted to try this, and even with those who were too young to know, she had supporters. It wouldn't be easy, but she wasn't alone.

He can't, but he can make my life difficult. He already is.

I'll protect you, whatever happens.

She smiled, showing her teeth. *I know. I would have hesitated to ask Sheldon to stay otherwise, but I know you'll always be there, both for him and for me.*

That hit too close to home for Morven to be comfortable with. He wanted to be close to Sheldon, but he wasn't sure Sheldon would allow him to, or that he would stay.

Things were getting complicated, both for the queen and for Morven, but there was nothing they could do but ride it out and wait for what would happen next.

Sheldon stared at Blake's phone. He'd lost his sometime between when he was abducted by Blake's old boss and when he'd been rescued, but he didn't miss it. He'd managed to call his job to tell them he was taking several days off, and that was the only important phone call he'd had to make. He didn't have friends to reassure, pets to care about or a significant other.

Well, apart from Morven.

He didn't know what he and Morven were, though. They hadn't talked about it, but eventually, they would have to. Blake was right, though. Sheldon needed to make a decision about staying or leaving before he started anything with Morven. It was both for his sake and Morven's, and he wanted them both to be happy. He suspected neither of them would be if he left, but then he'd always leaned toward staying. The only thing that stopped him was his parents, which was why he was about to call them.

He hoped they would want him to go back and that they were worried. It was what any good parents would do, but they'd never been good parents. They wouldn't have kicked Blake out if they had been.

Sheldon needed to do this, though. He needed to give them one last chance.

He snatched the phone, sat up in his nest, and dialed the number he knew from memory. It was his father's cell phone, and usually, he was the one to answer. Today wasn't any different.

"Where the fuck have you been?" he asked.

Sheldon winced. "Hello to you too, Dad. I'm fine, thanks for asking."

"Don't get smart with me. Where have you been? You were supposed to call someone for the kitchen sink, but no one has come around yet, and it's even worse now. It's leaking water all over the place."

Sheldon closed his eyes and took a deep breath. He didn't want to snap. His father was angry, but maybe that was only because he didn't realize something had happened to Sheldon. "I'm sorry. I know I promised I would call, but I had a problem."

"What problem?"

Sheldon straightened. Maybe his father actually cared. "I was kidnapped."

There was a pause before his father laughed. "You think you're funny? That's not going to get you out of this. You promised you'd call someone, and I expect you to keep that promise."

"I know it's not funny because it's true. I was worried about Blake, and I decided to go to his job to see if I could find him. Something happened, and his boss kicked the shit out of me. I have two broken ribs."

"I'm not paying your hospital bill. It's your own fault for looking for him. You shouldn't have. He's not part of our family anymore."

Sheldon had enough. "How can you say that? He's never done anything to you."

"He dishonored me!"

Sheldon chuckled darkly. "You never had any honor to begin with. How could he dishonor you?"

"Don't you dare talk to me like that."

"I'm bisexual." It was the first time Sheldon said the words out loud. He'd tried to explain to Blake earlier, but Blake had only nodded and kept on smiling. He didn't care who Sheldon loved. He only cared about Sheldon.

Sheldon's father didn't.

"What did you just say?" he asked.

"You heard me. I'm bisexual. I like both men and women, and right now, I'm in a relationship with a man."

"You're lying."

"I'm not. I'm sorry if it makes you love me less, but I'm not hiding anymore. I always thought that what you did to Blake wasn't right, and I knew that if I told you about this, you would do the same to me."

"No son of mine is going to fuck a man!"

"What about being fucked by one?" Sheldon asked. He didn't wait for an answer. He already knew what his father would say, so he hung up.

He stared at the phone. He'd known this was how things would go, but against all odds, he'd hoped.

He'd been wrong.

His parents didn't care about him. Even after he'd explained he'd been kidnapped, the only thing his father had cared about was his kitchen sink. He'd almost exploded when Sheldon told him he was bisexual, and that was before Sheldon mentioned that he was in a relationship with a man.

Not that he was. He didn't know what he and Morven were, but they'd kissed, and he wanted to see where it would go. He was still a bit afraid of having sex with Morven, mostly because he didn't know whether or not he would be any good at it. He didn't have that much experience, even though he was over thirty, but more than that, it was Morven's body. Sheldon had no idea where to start, but he supposed he would find out eventually.

Sheldon didn't have anything to go back to. He'd known it, but now he had proof, and nothing kept him from making the decision anymore. He doubted his parents would want to see him ever again. The only things he would have to go back to his job and his empty apartment.

Could he really stay, though?

It wasn't just that he was afraid. It would be too easy for any dragon to hurt him. Still, from what Blake had told him and what he'd seen, he knew that most of them didn't care that he and Blake were there. A lot were obviously curious, but thankfully, they were keeping their distance. They seemed to understand that it was too soon, especially now that word had gotten around that Sheldon had been attacked. They were giving him space, and that gave him one more reason to want to stay.

He was out of place, though. He wasn't a dragon. No matter how curious they were about him, that was never going to change. What was he supposed to do if he moved here? There was Blake, of course, but Blake had his own life. He had Orran and Blue. He was starting to make friends with dragons. Sheldon felt like he would hold Blake back if he stayed, even though he knew Blake wouldn't see things that way. Blake wanted Sheldon to stay. He wanted them to be in each other's lives again, and Sheldon wanted the same thing. It would be impossible if he went back to the city.

He had a decision to make. It was a big one, one that would change the rest of his life, and he had to be careful. He had to consider the pros and cons, maybe make a list, even though he knew that made him a dork.

He leaned back against the blankets and pillows that made up his nest. In the mental columns, he could put being too easily killed by dragons as a con. Also, there was a plot to hurt him and Blake to get to the queen. If he stayed, it was something he would have to deal with. It probably meant he wouldn't be able to go around the palace on his own, and even going with just Blake was dangerous. There wasn't much they could do against a dragon, even if they were together. In the same column, he put having to learn a lot. He knew some things about dragons, but only what his schoolbooks had told him. Dragons were nothing like he'd expected, and he would have to relearn everything and be careful not to insult anyone or to do something he shouldn't do.

He had help when it came to that, though. That was in the pros. If he stayed, he could be with Blake. They could heal their relationship and become even closer than they'd been when they were young. Blake had Orran and his own life, but that didn't mean Sheldon couldn't be part of it.

Sheldon was also eager to learn more about dragons. He'd never been fascinated by them the way Blake had been as a kid, but he wanted to learn. He and Blake were the only humans to know dragons were shifters as far as Sheldon was aware, and it thrilled him.

In the pros column, of course, there was Morven. They hadn't had a moment to chat privately since the day Sheldon had been attacked, but not because he hadn't wanted to. Morven was busy. He was the head of security for the queen and had to deal with security for the entire palace. He'd also had to find the dragon who had attacked Sheldon, something Sheldon knew he'd done. That particular danger was over, but more would come.

Would the pros column be long enough for Sheldon to decide to stay, then?

Now that the dragon who had attacked Sheldon had been exiled, Morven wanted to tell Sheldon himself. He suspected he would have to explain what being exiled meant for a dragon, but he was ready to do just that. When it came to Sheldon, he was ready to do a lot.

It didn't surprise him anymore. Sheldon was important to him. He hadn't understood why Orran was so taken with Blake, but now he did. It had nothing to do with the fact that Blake was human. It had everything to do with the fact that Blake was Blake, though. Blake was someone Orran had fallen in love with, and what he was didn't matter.

The same went for Morven. He liked Sheldon because he was Sheldon, and the fact that he was human had nothing to do with it.

When he arrived at Orran's rooms, no one answered the front door. He didn't want to barge in, but he really did need to talk to Sheldon, and Orran had always had an open-door policy when it came to him and their few friends. Morven knew he wouldn't mind, so after knocking one last time, he pushed open the main door.

The room was empty, but he knew for sure that Sheldon was here. Blake had told him Sheldon was wary of leaving his guest room. He was understandably afraid, and Morven wished he could do more. Maybe knowing that the dragon who had attacked him had been exiled would help, which was why Morven was here.

"Sheldon?" he called out.

He heard a noise coming from the hallway that led to the guest room, but he waited where he was. Sheldon appeared, frowning. "Morven? Has something happened?"

"No. Well, yes, but nothing bad. Can I talk to you?"

Sheldon relaxed, and when he smiled, it was glorious. "Of course. Do you want to do this here, or come into the guest room?"

"The guest room would be fine, if it's okay with you." Morven wanted a little privacy. He didn't know what would happen to them in the future, but he felt like this next step would be a cornerstone of their future relationship—if they ended up having one.

"It is. As long as we can head out later. No offense to Blake, but I'd feel safer walking around with you than with him."

That didn't sit well with Morven. He knew why Sheldon was afraid, and he wanted to strangle Janek for terrorizing Sheldon. Just the thought made him feel hot with fury. He couldn't do that, though. What he *could* do was be there for Sheldon. "Actually, we could fly."

Sheldon's eyes widened. He hadn't flown since the day he'd arrived, and while Morven had been convinced that he didn't like it, maybe he'd been wrong.

"You would do that?"

"I'd do pretty much anything for you." Morven hadn't meant to say that out loud, but now, he had, and he didn't regret it.

Sheldon's cheeks pinked, and he looked away. "I don't know what to say."

"Just tell me you want to go fly."

"Of course I do. I love the palace, but I want out, at least for a bit."

"I know the perfect place. Dress warmly. Grab everything you think you're going to need for the next few hours."

Sheldon grinned and disappeared into the hallway. Morven didn't know what would happen between them, but he found himself relaxing. Whatever happened, he would be there for Sheldon.

Sheldon hadn't yet told the queen what he was planning on doing, but he would soon. He would have to. Whatever his decision was, Morven would support him.

He wanted Sheldon to stay, of course. He didn't know how it had happened, but he was falling in love with the human, and he wanted Sheldon to be part of his life. That would only happen if Sheldon stayed, and while Morven hoped he was giving him enough incentive for that to happen, he couldn't be sure. He wouldn't find out until Sheldon told the queen, but in the meantime, Morven would act as if Sheldon wasn't going anywhere.

Sheldon burst from the hallway, dressed in a coat Morven had seen on Blake. He looked down and shrugged. "I know it's too big for me, but it's not like I have anything of my own."

"You look perfect. Besides, you'll be warm. It's the only thing that matters."

Sheldon nodded. "Shall we head out?"

"You want me to shift here? I can carry you."

"Not yet. I'm pretty sure I won't be able to deal with the ramps, but in the meantime, I think walking will do me good."

They left Orran's rooms behind. They walked side by side, and Morven was happy to see that Sheldon was fairly relaxed. He still tensed every time a dragon crossed their path, though, and Morven knew he had to tell him about Janek. "We caught the dragon who attacked you."

Sheldon peeked at Morven. "I heard about that."

"He was exiled."

Sheldon frowned. "What does that mean exactly?"

"Well, you know there aren't many dragons left. All of us live in clans. Being together gives us the strength of numbers, and it's easier to defend ourselves. It's why the entire Ogorth clan lives in the palace. It takes a lot of guards to defend, but considering it's dug into a mountain, it's also fairly easy. Being exiled from the clan means that Janek will be alone. He will have to defend himself. He won't have anyone at his back, and he'll be vulnerable. He's also lost the only family he has. Now no clan will want him, not once the word spreads."

Sheldon grimaced. "I know I shouldn't feel sorry for him considering what he did, but I do."

"I understand. You're a kindhearted man, and I'm not surprised you feel that way. The fact that Janek was exiled doesn't just have to do with you, though. He attacked you, and he hurt you, but he also went against the queen's orders. He attacked one of her guests and defied her. That's why she had to exile him."

"He can never come back?"

"No."

They reached the main room, and Sheldon looked down. "I think you have to shift now."

"I'll be happy to. Once I'm in my dragon form, climb onto my back."

"I will." Sheldon hesitated. "Thanks for telling me all of this. I needed an explanation. I don't want to feel like it's my fault that Janek was exiled."

"It's not. He knew what he was doing. He and others are working against the queen, and she has to be extremely careful."

"Yet she allowed me and Blake to stay."

"Because she wants things to change. She has the opportunity to have dragons and humans live together in peace. It means a lot to some dragons, including her. It won't be easy, but she's convinced about what she's doing."

Sheldon nodded. They were done talking, so Morven shifted and waited for him to climb onto his back. Once Sheldon was settled, Morven twisted his head to look at him, winked, and took flight.

Sheldon yelped, but he was holding on tightly. Morven flew up, landing once he reached the area that would lead to the outside pad. He had to walk there, but it was only a short walk. As soon as they reached the pad, he took to the air again. This time, Sheldon didn't scream. When Morven risked taking a peek at him, he was grinning like a loon, his eyes closed, his hair all over the place.

Morven headed toward the lake. It was the first place in which he'd realized he might be interested in Sheldon, and he hoped it would give Sheldon good memories.

The weather had gotten better, so hopefully, they would be able to sit on the grass and talk some more. The lake was isolated. A lot of dragons went there during the summer, but now it was autumn, and they tended to keep to the palace. That would give Morven and Sheldon privacy, which was something they sorely needed.

If Sheldon decided to stay, things would have to change. He couldn't live with his brother forever, and frankly, Morven would rather he not. He wanted to have time and space to see Sheldon and to get to know him better. Sheldon hadn't decided yet, though, and Morven needed to stop worrying about it.

When he landed, he turned around to make sure Sheldon was okay. To his delight, Sheldon was grinning at him.

"You chose this place on purpose, didn't you?" he asked.

Morven huffed. He couldn't answer, but he wanted to.

Luckily, Sheldon understood what his problem was and slid off his back. He stretched, and Morven took a moment to look at him before shifting. "I did," he confirmed.

"Thank you. I needed this."

"I know you don't love living in the palace."

"I don't, but it's because I'm not sure I'm safe there. You might have taken care of one of the dragons who wasn't happy about my presence, but I'm sure there are others."

Morven couldn't lie. "There are."

"I suppose I'll have to learn to deal with that knowledge."

He looked around, carefully choosing a spot before sitting. Morven went to sit next to him, knowing that if Sheldon needed space, he would demand it.

"You care about me, don't you?" Sheldon asked after a while.

"I thought it was obvious."

Sheldon shrugged. "It kind of is, but I wanted to be sure."

"You only have to ask. Anytime you want to know something, say the words. I'll answer as best as I can."

Sheldon stared for a moment. "What do you want? I know you said you didn't want to influence my decision whether or not to stay, but if I stay, what do you want from me?"

Morven still wasn't sure it was a good idea to say the words out loud, but Sheldon deserved to know. "If you stay, I want what Orran and Blake have."

"And you want that with me?"

"No, I want that with your cousin. Of course I want it with you."

Sheldon glared playfully. "You're not as funny as you seem to think you are." His expression turned more serious. "But thanks for telling me."

"I don't want to influence your decision."

"But don't you see? You already did, even when I didn't know you wanted this. I still have a hard time believing that a dragon would want me, but I know you're not lying."

"I'm not. I want you more than I've ever wanted anyone."

"I'm sure you think you do."

Morven reached for Sheldon. He took his hand in his and pulled until Sheldon had to lean closer. Morven hadn't been planning on anything when he'd started moving, but now, he hooked his arms around Sheldon and hauled him up. Sheldon squeaked, but before he could protest, Morven had him straddling his lap. They were facing each other, and Sheldon's cheeks were pink. He was adorable.

"I *know* I do. I don't know why it happened or how, but it doesn't matter. I want you in my life, Sheldon. I want you in my nest."

Sheldon's eyes were wide, but he smiled wickedly as he rocked his hips forward. "I can feel that."

"This is nothing next to what you'll feel if you continue."

Sheldon's rhythm faltered, but only for a second. "I think I'm ready to find out."

The words were stunning, but not as much as they would have been a little while ago. Morven already knew Sheldon wanted him. Now, they only had to do something about it. "You're sure?"

"I wouldn't say it if I weren't." Then Sheldon kissed Morven.

Morven wasn't about to protest. Sheldon knew what he was doing, obviously, and Morven wanted it as much as he did. He kissed Sheldon back, putting all his feelings into the kiss, hoping Sheldon would understand. They weren't at the stage where they could tell each other what they felt yet, but they could speak through their actions.

"I want to apologize preemptively if I do something I shouldn't do," Sheldon said when they separated. He was panting and staring at Morven as if Morven was the most precious thing in the world.

Morven wasn't used to being looked at that way, and it made something in his stomach churn. "You'll be perfect, whatever you do."

Sheldon snorted. "I doubt that's the case, but sure. Let's go with that."

Morven kissed him again. He hadn't expected this to happen, but now that it was, he yearned to feel more of Sheldon's body against his. He pushed his hands under Sheldon's coat and sweater, grinning when Sheldon shuddered. This probably wasn't the best place to do this, whatever they were about to do, but neither of them was willing to stop.

"I wish I could get naked with you," Sheldon murmured.

"I want to touch all of you."

"*I* am naked. You can."

Sheldon laughed. "As long as you won't be cold."

"How could I be cold when you'll be keeping me warm?"

Sheldon shook his head. "You're a smooth talker."

"Only for you."

"I'm pretty sure that's not true."

Morven didn't want Sheldon to be able to think, so instead of answering, he reached for Sheldon's jeans. The material was rough, and he wasn't sure why humans willingly wore it, but he supposed it had helped keep Sheldon warm as they flew. Right now, though, it was keeping what Morven wanted from him—a partially naked Sheldon. Morven fumbled with the button keeping the jeans fastened until Sheldon took pity and decided to help.

Morven wanted Sheldon naked, but the sight of his cock springing up when he pushed his jeans apart and another piece of clothing down almost made up for it. It looked nothing like Morven's, but then, Sheldon looked nothing like Morven. His cock was pink, with a darker head. The form was similar to Morven's, but the color was off, although Morven supposed it was normal for Sheldon.

"I'm going to start thinking there's something wrong with it if you keep staring," Sheldon said.

He sounded amused, so Morven knew he wasn't behaving too badly. "The differences between us are fascinating."

Sheldon's gaze dropped to Morven's groin. His cock had slid out of his pouch, so Sheldon could see what he had to offer. "You can touch," Morven said. After all, he was touching Sheldon.

"I want to do much more than just touching."

"Do whatever you want. I'm yours to touch and take."

Sheldon's gaze flickered down again. "You're serious about that?"

Morven wasn't surprised Sheldon was asking. He'd talked to Orran a bit about humans, and he knew they tended to be more binary than dragons. They expected certain people to act a certain way, and while the same went for dragons in public settings, it didn't in bed — or on the shore of a lake. "I am."

Sheldon swallowed heavily and reached for Morven's cock. Morven didn't want to rush him, but he needed more, so he shifted their position until Sheldon's cock pressed against his pouch. It made it hard for Sheldon to touch him, but he didn't complain. Instead, he moved, too, and ended up between Morven's legs.

He looked at Morven. His pupils were huge, showing how aroused he was. "Do I need to, uh, do anything? Like, lube?"

"No. I'm ready for you." Was he ever. He couldn't wait. He didn't know what would happen between them, if Sheldon would stay or go, but they would always have the memories of this.

Sheldon still looked hesitant, but he didn't ask if Morven was sure. Instead, he moved back just enough to grab his cock and aimed it at Morven's pouch. Morven waited, holding his breath. He hadn't done this in a while. He was too busy to dedicate time to a new relationship or even just to sex, or that was what he'd told himself. Clearly, he had the time for Sheldon.

The head of Sheldon's cock breached the pouch, and Morven had to release the breath. He screwed his eyes shut, focusing on the pleasure until he realized Sheldon had stopped moving. He fluttered his eyes open to look at him. "What is it?"

"You deserve more than me taking you on the shore of a lake."

Morven had no idea where this was coming from. "I deserve you. That's it. I'm fine with anything, as long as it's with you."

Sheldon stared at Morven for a moment longer. Then, he pushed.

Morven was warm and soft, and surprisingly slick, considering they weren't using lube. All coherent thoughts flew right out of Sheldon's mind as soon as he was fully inside Morven. He could feel Morven tighten around him, but also Morven's cock rubbing against his, and it was incredibly arousing. Sheldon had never felt anything like this. He'd already been addicted to Morven before. This wasn't going to help.

He didn't want to disappoint Morven, but the sensations were maddening. They were new, yet familiar, and Morven was beautiful under Sheldon. He wished he could have given Morven more, but he'd have time to do that once he fully moved into the palace. They'd find a way to make this work, and Sheldon would cherish Morven.

"Come inside me," Morven murmured.

Sheldon bit his lower lip so hard he could taste blood. "Stop saying that, because it'll happen right away if you continue."

Morven grinned. "That's fine with me." Then he surged up and twisted them at the same time.

Sheldon didn't know how he did it, but he managed to keep his cock inside Morven as Morven flipped them. He didn't have much time to think about it, because Morven kissed him while grinding their groins together. Sheldon felt like he slipped even deeper inside Morven, although he didn't think that was possible. Whatever the case, Morven's actions had the effect he'd been looking for—Sheldon thrust up as Morven pushed down and squeezed around him.

Sheldon clung to Morven's hips. He only briefly thought about the fact that if he left bruises, everyone would be able to see them. Morven did something with his hips, a twist and push, and Sheldon couldn't think about anything. He bit his lower lip so he wouldn't cry out, even though they were alone. His cock jerked inside Morven, and Sheldon did as Morven had told him — he came inside of him.

He only took a few seconds to bask in the pleasure before reaching for Morven's cock. He jerked it as Morven continued grinding on his cock, which thankfully, wasn't yet softening. It wouldn't be long, though, so Sheldon did his best to give Morven pleasure. Morven shuddered and dropped on top of Sheldon. Sheldon felt Morven's cock spurt between them, and he used his free arm to wrap around Morven's waist and hold him close.

"Feeling better?" Morven murmured against the skin of Sheldon's neck.

"I do. Was it okay?" Sheldon hoped that was the case. If not, he wouldn't mind trying again and again until he nailed it.

Morven tilted his head so he could look at Sheldon. "Would you believe me if I told you it was perfect?"

Sheldon snorted. "Nothing is ever perfect."

"Maybe not, but we can try."

Sheldon grinned. "That's what I was thinking." Then he stopped thinking at all, because Morven kissed him and pressed closer, and Sheldon had better things to focus on.

CHAPTER EIGHT

Sheldon watched the dragons chase each other in the air. He couldn't help but smile at the sight. They were behaving more like children than young adults right now.

He still couldn't believe he'd been invited to watch their game. He hadn't known what to expect, and he didn't want to offend anyone, but he thought they looked like overgrown puppies. They were throwing a ball at each other, flying to catch it, then throwing it again. They were playing at the landing pad, because it was the biggest area in which they could do this, and Sheldon wondered if they were allowed. It looked like this place had a precise purpose, and playing ball definitely wasn't that.

"You're more relaxed," Blake said, knocking their shoulders together.

They were both wrapped in a blanket. They needed it, since winter was quickly coming. The dragons didn't seem to have a problem with it, but it might be a problem for Sheldon and Blake with all the palace openings. Sheldon supposed it was one more thing to worry about now that he'd decided to move. The palace wasn't built for humans, but the queen had promised to try to fix as many things as she could to make them comfortable.

"It helps that I'm not in pain," he told his brother.

Blake grimaced. "I can't believe you were attacked inside the palace. I knew the queen was having problems, but I never realized it was this bad."

Sheldon wasn't surprised. His brother often only saw what

he wanted to see, and in this case, it had been an idyllic life with dragons. Blake was isolated. From what Sheldon had seen, he didn't spend much time with dragons outside of Orran, Morven, the rest of their team. And of course, Blue and the people who worked around him. Sheldon, on the other hand, wanted more. That was why he'd started taking walks around the palace with Morven. He wanted dragons to see him and to realize he wasn't a threat.

The fact that he was dating their head of security probably helped.

Sheldon had a hard time wrapping his mind around that. He and Morven were together, and he'd never been so happy. If someone had told him he would be dating a dragon a month ago, he would have thought they were bananas. Instead, he actually was dating a dragon, and what a dragon Morven was.

It wasn't just that, though. Now that people saw Sheldon more often, he'd noticed that some dragons were relaxing and were more eager to talk to him. From what he'd been told, they were mostly young ones — dragons who, like the queen, thought that dragons and humans should peacefully live together. Sheldon was aware that he and Blake would have a harder time convincing the older dragons.

They still remembered how awful it had been when humans had decided dragons needed to die and when they'd hunted them until only a handful remained. It was then that they'd retreated into their palaces and started a hidden life. Having Sheldon and Blake there gave the older dragons bad memories while it gave the youngest ones hope that one day, they would be able to leave their palaces and travel the world without having to fear that someone would kill them.

When the game ended, Sheldon had no idea who had won — if anyone had. It didn't matter. The dragons had fun, and they shifted as they landed, pushing each other around and laughing. Sheldon wasn't quite part of their group, and he never would be since he wasn't a dragon, but this was a start, and he made sure to smile at them and congratulate them.

He and Blake headed back to Blake's rooms. That was something else Sheldon would have to deal with. He didn't want to stay with his brother and Orran for much longer, but he also wasn't sure that asking the queen for a room was the best idea. He felt safer here, and even though the dragon who had attacked him had been kicked out, he knew there were others waiting for the right moment.

There was also the detail of a job. What was he supposed to do now that he'd decided to stay? He was great with computers, but did the dragons need him? It was the only thing he could do, and he knew he'd have to talk to the queen about it. He might have agreed to stay, and he might be eager, but it didn't mean he didn't have doubts.

"I'm glad you're not going anywhere," Blake said as they walked. "I would have missed you."

Because Sheldon would never have been able to see Blake again if he'd left. "I couldn't do it. You're my favorite brother."

Blake snorted. "I'm your only brother."

"I suppose that helps." Sheldon grinned. "I'm glad I'm not going anywhere, too. I want us to have a real relationship, not what we had in the past few years. I know it was my fault, but—"

"Don't even start. You were trying to make both me and our parents happy, and I don't resent you for that. I could have told you that you wouldn't succeed with them, but you needed to see it for yourself. Now that you have, you know they don't deserve all the time and effort you put into them."

He wasn't wrong.

They turned the corner, and Sheldon's step faltered. They

were almost at Orran's rooms, and he hadn't expected to be attacked here.

He'd been wrong.

Three dragons were standing in the middle of the hallway, blocking Blake and Sheldon's way. One of them was in his human form, while the other two were in their dragon forms behind him.

Sheldon tried to put himself in front of Blake, but Blake was having none of that. He pushed Sheldon back and faced the dragons. "What do you want?" he asked. His voice was stern, but it wasn't offensive.

The expression of the dragon in his human form twisted. "For you to die."

Well, Sheldon supposed he couldn't have been clearer.

"Orran will kick your ass if you as much as touch one hair on my head," Blake warned.

"I'm pretty sure he knows that and that he doesn't care," Sheldon murmured.

Blake shook his head. "*I* don't care. They have to know that they won't get away with this."

The dragon grinned wickedly. "We will if there's nothing of you to find."

That much was true, too. Orran and Morven would be all over the place if Sheldon and Blake vanished, but if they couldn't find them, they would never know what happened. The easiest way to do that was to make their bodies disappear, and those dragons could burn them to a crisp. Even if they didn't, it would only take one step for Blake and Sheldon to be stomped to death, and that would be it for them.

The dragon stepped closer. Sheldon followed his movements, moving back and pulling Blake along with him. Even though Blake was trying to protect him, he was only human. There wasn't much he could do against dragons.

The dragon was still grinning, and he wasn't the only one.

The other two were smiling, too, exposing their teeth and giving Sheldon a hint as to what they were planning. However they died, Sheldon and Blake weren't leaving this place on their feet, not today.

Sheldon was still going to try. He grabbed Blake's hand and turned around, ready to run, only to find the other side of the hallway blocked, too. A sob escaped him, but before he could break down, the two dragons on that side shifted, allowing a third one in his human form to pass.

It was Morven.

Sheldon's knees almost buckled. He had to lean against the wall, but thankfully, he didn't fall on his face. "How did you know?" he asked as Morven walked past him.

"We suspected someone was going to attack you again. We were right." His expression was grim, and while Sheldon wanted to smooth it out, he knew it wasn't his place. Right now, Morven wasn't his boyfriend. He was the head of security. He was the one who would arrest the three dragons and make sure they paid for what they'd almost done.

The problem was that the dragons wouldn't allow Morven to take them away peacefully. The one who had attacked Sheldon previously had left of his own will. These three wouldn't. Sheldon knew as soon as the one in front shifted and opened his mouth to spit fire at Morven.

Sheldon held his breath. He knew Morven was a fighter, but he wanted a long and happy life with him.

He wasn't sure he would get it.

Morven had known something like this would happen, but it didn't change how terrified he was. He and the others had been following the brothers around the palace, keeping an eye on them. Morven could and should have assigned the task to someone else, but he had to keep Sheldon safe himself. Now, he was relieved he had.

He wasn't surprised at the fire coming toward him, and he shifted in the blink of an eye. The fire hit his skin, and while it burned to the point of pain, it would have been worse if he'd been in his human form. This way, he wouldn't get burned.

He roared, the walls shaking around him, and threw himself at the dragon.

The dragon tried to run away, but he couldn't. Another two dragons stood behind him, blocking the hallway. It was what they'd intended for Blake and Sheldon, but now, it put them in trouble as the three of them tried to scramble over each other to run.

Morven jumped. He landed on top of the dragon he was chasing, pinning him to the ground, and dug his claws into the dragon's wings. They were folded, but it would still hurt, and the dragon tried to buck him off. Instead of going with the movement, Morven leaned down and bit onto the back of the dragon's neck.

The dragon froze. He knew that if Morven tightened his hold even more, he could snap his neck.

Morven waited. He trusted Octavia and Hogan to take care of the other two. Stalin was around as well, in case they needed more help, but the space was tight, and they would probably trip over each other's tails if he tried to intervene.

To Morven's surprise, the dragon under him shifted. "Kill me," he muttered.

Morven was tempted. The dragon had threatened the man he loved. He deserved to die, and not only for that. He'd gone against the queen's orders, and he no doubt worked for Caven. If Morven hadn't suspected something like this would happen, the situation could have gotten out of hand.

Instead of doing what the dragon wanted, Morven shifted, too. He couldn't keep on biting the dragon's neck in his human form, but he could slam the dragon against the wall, face first. He didn't think anyone would care if the dragon's cheek was scraped.

Morven leaned closer, using his body to press the dragon against the wall. "Who ordered you to do this?"

The dragon shook his head. "No one. We're not happy with the humans being here, and we wanted them to know it. We weren't going to hurt them."

"Why did you go for them the way you did, then?"

"They're always surrounded by people. We felt it was the only way to get them alone."

"You're lying. You wanted to kill them. You were ordered to."

"I don't know what you're talking about."

These three weren't going to be exiled like Janek. Morven wanted answers, and he would get them.

He turned around to see that Slavin had arrived, along with several guards. "Take the three of them down to the cells."

"Do I get to interrogate them?" Hogan asked.

Morven almost winced at the deep cut on Hogan's arm. "You're going to need a healer first," he pointed out.

Hogan grinned. "I can deal with it. It's just a scratch."

A scratch made by a dragon claw, which meant it was deep and bleeding. "It's an order. See a healer. Once that's done, you can interrogate those three all you want."

Hogan looked at Morven. "You're not going to do it yourself?"

"Eventually. Right now, though, I have something else to focus on."

Morven turned his attention to the brothers. They were standing against the wall, pressed against each other. Sheldon looked like he was freaking out, while Blake was afraid, but not as badly.

Morven didn't want to scare Sheldon even more, so he

moved slowly when he neared them. "Are you two okay?" he asked.

Blake grimaced. "We've been better, but we weren't wounded. Is Hogan going to be okay?"

"He will. To him, it's just a scratch."

Sheldon made a strangled noise. "Just a scratch? He's bleeding all over the place."

"He's had much worse." From the way Sheldon paled, Morven wasn't sure those were the right words to reassure him.

Sheldon had just made the decision to stay, and Morven had been over the moon happy. Now, he couldn't help but wonder if Sheldon was going to change his mind.

No one would blame him if he did. Sheldon couldn't stay at the palace until this situation was over. It was too dangerous for him and Blake. But Blake spent most of his time with dragons Morven trusted. He took care of Blue, and he was usually around guards. Sheldon, on the other hand, didn't have an official job. He was free to roam the palace, although as far as Morven knew, he hadn't yet. He was a prisoner in his room, even though no one wanted him to be.

"Blake!" someone yelled.

Morven turned to see Orran running toward them. He was frantic, and when he got to them, he pulled Blake into his arms. They wrapped around each other, and Morven turned his attention back to Sheldon.

Would he be allowed to do that? Was it something Sheldon wanted? Or would he be afraid of Morven? Morven wouldn't be surprised. He'd been attacked by dragons twice, and Morven was a dragon.

He had to try, though. If Sheldon decided to leave because of what had just happened, Morven wanted more time with him. He gently touched Sheldon's arm, and when Sheldon looked at him, opened his wide. He smiled when Sheldon pushed away from the wall and twined his arms around him. He relaxed, even though he knew the situation wasn't over. He and Sheldon needed to talk, and even though Morven wished he could wait, they needed to talk now.

"I'll walk you back to your room," he murmured.

Sheldon nodded. "I've had enough exploration for today."

"I'm sorry this happened to you."

Sheldon looked up at Morven. "I'm sorry, too. It wasn't your fault, though."

It hadn't been, but everyone would understand if Sheldon decided he'd rather go back to his life in the city. This place was dangerous for him, and he'd already been attacked twice. Morven had been there both times, but he might not be the next time, and he didn't know what he would do if something happened to Sheldon.

He left Octavia in charge of making sure the three dragons made it to the cells in one piece. He couldn't trust Hogan with it, not when Hogan would have fun tearing the dragons' heads off and playing ball with them. He and Sheldon walked slowly. They wouldn't have been able to go faster, not when they were still half wrapped around each other. They were silent as they reached Orran and Blake's rooms, and they went straight to Sheldon's guest room. Morven knew that Orran and Blake would want some time to themselves, too, and he wanted to give them the time and space.

"You sure you're okay?" he asked Sheldon once the door was closed behind them.

Sheldon nodded. "I'm fine. They didn't hurt me."

Morven swallowed. "They didn't, but it was close."

"What's going on? Why did they attack? I know a lot of dragons aren't happy about my and Blake's presence here, but this felt like more. They wanted to hurt us, even though we didn't do anything to them."

Morven sighed. "It's twofold. They don't like you being

here, and they wouldn't hesitate to kill you to make sure you weren't anymore, but they're also trying to destabilize the queen. Her cousin wants to take her place on the throne, and he'll only be able to do that if he manages to topple her. He's using your presence here both to show other dragons that she's not thinking straight, but also to show that she can't protect you and that as such, she's not a good leader."

Sheldon frowned. "But she is. Anyone else would have left me with Hans, but instead, she sent an entire team to save me, even though she didn't know me. She offered me a place to stay and a home."

"That's why most dragons in the clan love her. She's a hard worker, and she truly cares about all of us. She puts the clan's happiness before its prestige and power. She wants to make a difference, and if she has the opportunity, she will."

Sheldon slowly nodded. "I see. Well, the situation is more complicated than I thought, and I'm sorry I'm giving the queen this much work."

"Don't worry about it. She knew what she was doing when she asked you to stay." And Sheldon had agreed. But now, he might change his mind, and Morven had never been so terrified. He would face a hundred dragons every day to save Sheldon, but he never wanted to be in this situation again.

Sheldon felt better now that he knew it wasn't actually about him, not entirely. Sure, some dragons weren't happy to have him and Blake at the palace, but mostly, they were being used to show that the queen wasn't a good leader.

Knowing that solidified his choice of staying. If he left, everyone would know it was because he'd been attacked not once, but twice. They would no doubt use that against the queen.

Most people would have thought it wasn't his business,

and they would be right. He wanted that to change, though. If he became a part of the clan, the queen would be his queen, too. He wanted her to continue being on the throne because she was a good queen. The people who thought otherwise were delusional, and Sheldon wouldn't allow them to run him out of the palace.

He turned to Morven. "I want to go to the city." He needed to get his things and move into his own room, if possible. He loved his brother, but he'd stumbled onto him and Orran getting frisky one too many times.

Morven's expression tightened. "Of course. I understand. The palace is dangerous, and no one will expect you to say, not when you've already been attacked twice."

Sheldon cocked his head. "What did you hear that I didn't say?"

Morven blinked. "You just said you wanted to go back to the city. You're leaving."

Sheldon almost rolled his eyes, but he understood why Morven thought that. "I already told you and the queen I was staying. I'm not changing my mind."

"You're not? You just said you wanted to go back to the city."

"I said I wanted to go to the city. I need to pack up my things and get them here. I want to wear my own clothes, not Blake's borrowed ones. I don't have a lot, but it's my stuff, and I want it. I think it would help me feel more settled here."

Morven slowly nodded. "No one would think badly of you if you wanted to leave, though. You don't have to stay just because you think it's the right thing to do. It's dangerous, and I don't want you to get hurt."

Sheldon moved closer, pressing his hand against Morven's smooth chest. "But if I stay, you'll protect me, right?"

Morven raised his hand to catch Sheldon's, squeezing the back of it. "I'll always protect you, whether you stay or go."

He paused and smiled. "It will be harder if you go, but I'm nothing but determined."

"You won't have to be. I'm not going anywhere, not for the long run."

Morven kept staring, and Sheldon waited. If Morven had more questions, he would be more than happy to answer them, especially if they stayed so close to each other.

They were still trying to find a way to make their relationship work. It wasn't easy, not when Sheldon felt lost and Morven was crazy busy. Hopefully, Sheldon would be able to get a job with the dragons. He couldn't imagine not doing anything day in and day out, and he knew it would drive him nuts. Even if he had to do something that wasn't related to computers, it would be fine with him, as long as it was something. He didn't like feeling like he wasn't contributing, not when the clan was feeding him and giving him a safe place.

Well, relatively safe.

"I don't understand," Morven said. "You've already been attacked twice, so you know you're not safe here. Furthermore, you have a life in the city. I know you have your parents, even though they're not good people. But even if you don't take them into consideration, you have your apartment and your job. Why would you want to move here?"

Sheldon rolled his eyes. "It's almost as if you're trying to convince me to go."

"I'm not. If I had my way, I would lock you in my room and never allow you to leave. But I don't want you to regret making this decision."

"I won't. I've had time to think about it, and I know I'm making the right choice. But you're right. I have a job in the city, and it's kind of scary to leave it behind, especially when I don't know if I'll be able to find a new one here. Still, losing my job is worth being here with you and my brother. It's worth living with dragons and discovering a whole new world."

"What about your parents?"

Sheldon shrugged. "It hurts. I won't deny it does." He'd tried calling his father again, but he hadn't answered. Sheldon had no doubt that as far as his parents were concerned, they had no children. "I always tried to be the perfect son, since Blake was the black sheep of the family. Even before he came out to them, he was treated differently because he didn't go to college. They thought his life was a disaster, and they never missed a chance to berate him for it. It's why I work so hard. I wanted them to be proud of me. Now I know that it was pointless, because the fact that I'm in love with you is enough for them to decide they don't want me. It's not right. Who I love doesn't change who I am."

"As long as you won't regret it."

"I probably will eventually. Living here isn't going to be easy. I'm not even talking about the attacks. The palace is freezing."

Morven chuckled and pulled Sheldon closer to him, wrapping his arms around him. "I'll keep you warm."

"Unfortunately, you can't be with me twenty-four seven. Besides, I'm sure that eventually we're going to fight and yell at each other, and I won't want to see you for a few hours. It's what every normal couple does, and I'm kind of looking forward to it."

Morven arched a brow. "You're looking forward to fighting with me?"

"I'm looking forward to having a life with you. If I went back, I would end up hating myself and my bland life. I want more, and I want *you*."

"I'm kind of terrified that you're going to resent me eventually," Morven confessed.

"I won't. Your presence here is part of the reason I decided to stay, but it's not the main reason. I want this life. I hope it will come with fewer attacks, but I'll deal with it if they happen. I'm never going back to my boring life in the city. I'm done with that."

Sheldon had never thought it possible, but he had a new life, and he didn't want to lose it. What more could he want? He had a home, a family, Blake, and now, Morven. They wouldn't use him the way his parents had. It would take work, and Sheldon wasn't lying when he said he'd probably regret staying a few times at least, but he could deal with it.

He could deal with a lot if it meant having this new life — and Morven.

Morven needed to stop trying to convince Sheldon to leave, especially since it wasn't what he wanted. Sheldon had said he wouldn't regret staying, not beyond fleeting moments, and Morven should believe him. He was an adult, and he was making his own decisions. Morven should trust him to know what he was doing.

Sheldon knew what staying would imply. He knew there was a possibility he could be attacked again, and that the next time, he might not be as lucky as he'd been today.

He was staying anyway. Being at the palace and living with dragons was worth it, and no matter what Sheldon said, Morven hoped he was part of the reasons Sheldon was staying.

"I'll go with you to the city," he declared.

"No offense, but I'm pretty sure my neighbors would notice a dragon packing up my stuff and taking it away, even if you're in your human form. You're not exactly ordinary looking."

"I'll find a way. I want to help you."

Sheldon grinned. "And you want to make sure I don't change my mind."

Morven felt sick at the thought. "Do you think you will?"

Sheldon shook his head and kissed Morven. "No. Once I'm here, you're not getting rid of me. I hope you're aware of that."

"It's more than fine with me."

They gave Orran and Blake plenty of time to talk, and possibly, to do other things. Morven had been terrified for Sheldon, even though he'd expected something like this to happen. Spending time alone with him to cuddle and talk about what their future would be like was heaven. He knew the same had to go for Orran. They both needed to reassure themselves that the men they loved weren't going.

Morven didn't know when it had happened. He'd realized he was in love with Sheldon one day, and there had been nothing he could do to change that. Sheldon was part of his life now, which was both terrifying and elating. Sheldon could easily get hurt, but Morven would make sure he didn't. They were in this together, and together, they would build a life. Morven wouldn't allow anything different to happen.

When they headed back to the main room, Blake's hair was mussed, and there was a hickey on his neck, but both he and Orran looked more relaxed. Blake rushed to Sheldon to make sure he was okay, and Morven headed toward his friend.

"You're both okay?" he asked.

Orran nodded. "It was the scariest thing I've ever done, and I was head of security for years. Willingly putting him in danger, though . . ."

"You didn't put him in danger. The dragons who attacked him did."

"But we knew something like this would happen, yet we let them roam the palace on their own, without protection."

"They did have protection. We were there."

Orran scowled. "You were. I had to stay back as if I didn't know how to fight."

"You're not a fighter anymore, though. You're Blue's tutor, and I couldn't put you at risk. Besides, things went well. Both Blake and Sheldon are fine, and Sheldon decided to stay." Morven beamed. "He wants to go to the city to pack up his things and move here indefinitely."

"I suppose that's good considering the situation. I understand why you didn't tell me, but I'm a little hurt."

Morven frowned. "What are you talking about? You knew Sheldon wanted to stay. I thought he might have changed his mind since he's been attacked twice, but he hasn't."

Orran's eyes were wide. "You haven't noticed?"

"Noticed what?"

Orran pointed at Morven's stomach. Morven looked down, not knowing what to expect, and froze. There, in the middle of his stomach, was a dark green line. It ran from his sternum to his pouch, and as much as he wanted to, Morven couldn't ignore it.

He looked at Orran again. He couldn't say anything. He wasn't even sure he could still think.

"I take it that it wasn't on purpose?" Orran asked gently.

Morven shook his head. "I didn't even notice. There was so much going on."

"You would have felt it, though."

Morven thought about it. It had been easy to ignore the signs that he was fertile. He'd felt weird, had hot flashes and stomach pains, and he hadn't been sleeping well, but he'd ascribed all of that to how stressed he was. He couldn't believe he hadn't thought for one second that he was in his fertile period.

And now, he was pregnant.

He looked at Sheldon, who was chatting with Blake. He wasn't even sure Sheldon knew this was possible. Orran had to explain to Blake that when it came to dragons, both males and females could carry young. Their fertile periods only came once every several years, which was one of the reasons there were so few of them left. Blake had taken it well, but then, he hadn't gotten Orran pregnant.

Sheldon had, though. He was going to be a father, and he didn't even know it was possible.

Orran cleared his throat to get Blake's attention. "I know you told Sheldon about sex with dragons."

Sheldon's cheeks became so red that his face looked like it was about to explode. Morven wondered if their child would have the same reaction to embarrassment and if their cheeks would turn red, too. Would they have Sheldon's hair? His knobby knees? His stubbornness and strength?

Blake grinned. "I did. He was interested in Morven, and he wanted to know if it would be possible for them to do the nasty."

Sheldon slapped his brother's arm. "Don't call it that. Nothing Morven and I do is nasty."

"Did you also tell him about dragons' fertility?" Orran asked, ignoring their bickering.

Blake frowned. "I didn't. I mean, he was asking about sex, not about how to get Morven pregnant." His eyes widened so much that Morven wouldn't have been surprised to see them pop out of his skull. "Wait. Is that what's happening? Is Morven pregnant?"

Morven sighed. He couldn't keep it a secret. Orran had noticed, which meant that others would, too. They'd start to congratulate him, and Sheldon would find out. Besides, Morven had to talk to the queen about it. He'd have to be more careful with the egg and the baby growing inside of him, and while he wasn't planning on stepping down from his role as head of security, he'd have to delegate some tasks.

"I'm confused," Sheldon said slowly. He was staring at Morven's stomach. "That line wasn't there before. I'm sure of it."

Morven stepped closer to him. He didn't want to freak Sheldon out, although he supposed it was too late for that. "I'm sorry. I didn't think to tell you this was a possibility."

Sheldon laughed hysterically. "A possibility? You mean Blake is right?"

"He is. Dragons, both male and female, aren't very fertile. It only happens once every few years, and while there are physical warning signs, there was so much happening that I dismissed them as exhaustion and worry." Sheldon was still staring, and Morven wondered if it was in horror or something else. Maybe not pleasure yet, but eventually?

"So you were fertile, and we had sex. I—I got you pregnant."

"You did." And Morven was getting worried. He wanted to give Sheldon time to wrap his mind around this, but he also wanted him to know that if he'd rather step away from the situation, Morven wouldn't hold it against him. His life was already changing so much. The last thing he probably needed was a dragon-human hybrid baby.

There was no way to know what would happen. Morven doubted it ever had, and he didn't like it. He wanted his and Sheldon's baby to be okay, but would they?

That was something he would have to worry about another time, though.

He cleared his throat. "This baby is yours, but you don't have to do anything."

Sheldon's eyes narrowed. "What do you mean?"

"This was a shock for you."

"As it was for you."

"Yes, but I knew I could get pregnant. I should have been more careful. I should have told you it was a possibility."

"Do you regret it?"

Morven pressed a hand against his stomach. "No." Not just because it was Sheldon's baby and he loved Sheldon, but also because for dragons, getting pregnant was a precious miracle. Even when they were fertile, they didn't always manage. Morven had, though, and he couldn't imagine not being happy about the baby.

"I don't know what to say." Sheldon shook his head. "I have no idea how to be a father."

"You don't have to be one if you're not comfortable."

Sheldon pointed at Morven. "Don't you dare. I'm in shock, and I've never had a good father role model, but it doesn't mean I don't want this baby." He paused and bit his lip. "You're going to have to walk me through this, though."

Morven moved closer to Sheldon and carefully wrapped his arms around him. When Sheldon didn't push him away, he relaxed and kissed Sheldon's temple. "We'll walk through it together. I've never been pregnant, so I'm not sure what to expect, either. We'll figure it out, though."

Sheldon looked up at Morven, and to Morven's surprise, he stroked his stomach. "Together."

Morven nodded. "Together."

CHAPTER NINE

Sheldon was going to be a father. He'd never thought some-thing like this would happen, although he supposed he should have. He was bisexual, after all, and since he'd never told his parents that he also liked men, they'd only ever seen him with women. It could have happened with any of them, but instead, it had happened with Morven.

Morven, who was very much male. Morven, who was pregnant anyway.

Sheldon tried to focus on the book in front of him, but the words didn't make sense to his overtired mind. Ever since he and Morven had found out they were expecting, Sheldon had been freaking out. It wasn't just because he never expected to be a father. There was also the fact that as far as anyone could remember, there had never been a human and dragon hybrid, not even when dragons and humans lived in peace. Even back then, dragons had kept their shifting secret to themselves, and they'd been wise to do so. That meant that no one knew what the baby would be like, or even if they would survive, and Sheldon was freaking out. He might not have been sure about it in the beginning, but now, he didn't want to lose the baby.

That was why he'd been going through all the books in the palace library since he and Morven had come back from the city. So far, he hadn't found anything, but he wasn't giving up.

He might never have expected to become a dad, but now he was, and he would make sure his son or daughter was okay. He would do anything to make that happen, including spending hours poring over old dusty books.

Hopefully, this was one of the ways he would be a better father than his own father. That scared him, too. He didn't know how to be a dad. His father had only ever scorned and used him and Blake, and Sheldon didn't want to do the same. He'd promised himself he wouldn't, but the fear was still there. He wasn't like his father, but he was still his father's son. Would he be as fucked-up as he was?

He rubbed his eyes, hoping that the gesture would make the book easier to read. It didn't, though. He knew he had to stop for tonight. Morven was probably already waiting for him in their rooms, and Sheldon couldn't wait to go back to him.

He'd moved in with Morven. It made sense, especially since they were expecting, but he and Morven were still trying to find their way around each other. They were in love, but they'd never lived together, and it was taking some getting used to. It *would* happen, though. Sheldon was excited about his new life, and especially so now that he was going to be a dad. It was terrifying in many ways, but also exhilarating.

Blake didn't miss a chance to tease Sheldon about it. He'd apologized for not telling Sheldon that it could happen, but Sheldon wasn't angry at him. He couldn't have predicted that Morven would be fertile right around the time he and Sheldon had sex. They'd just met, and from the sound of it, dragons were fertile only once every few years. What were the odds?

None of that mattered, not now that Sheldon had managed to wrap his mind around it. Male dragons could get pregnant. It wasn't a problem, not for Sheldon. What *was* a problem was not knowing what his and Morven's child would be like, or if they would have any kind of difficulties. Not even the healers had an answer to that, and Sheldon was freaking out.

"You should go home," a voice said behind him.

Sheldon jumped, relieved he wasn't drinking anything that could have spilled over the book. He turned around and glared at Hogan. "What are you doing here? This is the library, not the training room."

Luckily for him, Hogan didn't look offended. "I'm aware of that. I know what books are."

"Really? I wasn't sure you did since I've never seen you with one."

"That's because I'm too busy. Now that you got Morven pregnant, we all have to carry the weight in the team."

Morven had stepped back from his role as head of security. He still worked for the queen, and he would go back to the full-time job once he laid the egg—and wasn't that strange to think about—but for now, he was dividing the demands of the job between himself, Orran, and the rest of their teams. Octavia hadn't been happy about it, but she'd insisted on being part of it anyway. Hogan, on the other hand, seemed to have a lot of fun terrorizing younger guards. It was all in good fun, which was the only reason Sheldon didn't say anything about it. Hogan wouldn't really scare or hurt anyone, or at least, not anyone who wasn't dangerous to the clan.

Sheldon still wasn't sure what had happened to those three dragons, but after Hogan had taken care of them, no one was. They were probably still in the cells, but Sheldon wasn't about to ask. He didn't care, not after what they'd done.

"You should go home to him," Hogan said, his voice softer.

"I will. I was just looking up something."

"Everything will be fine. The two of you will have a strong and healthy baby, and you'll be happy."

Sheldon twisted in his chair so he could look at Hogan more fully. "I thought you didn't like me."

Hogan shrugged. "I never said I didn't like you."

"Fine. I thought you didn't like humans, then."

"I was hesitant about your presence here. I can't easily

forget what humans did to my family. I have to admit that you and your brother aren't as bad as I thought, though. You make Morven happy, and you're giving him a baby."

Sheldon felt his cheeks heat, but he didn't look away. "Thank you. This means a lot."

"Don't think I'll make a habit of spilling my feelings all over the place, though. Go to your man. I'll put away the books."

Sheldon obeyed. He did want to go back to Morven, and he could take the night off. He'd made it his job to go over as many books as possible while Morven was still pregnant, and he would continue doing so until they were sure their baby was okay. Everything else could wait, including finding a more permanent job with the clan.

"Thank you," he repeated as he passed by Hogan.

"Stop thanking me. As long as you make him happy, you're okay in my book."

That was much more than Sheldon had expected he would get, and he continued thinking about the conversation as he headed toward his and Morven's rooms. When he walked in, Morven was already there, sitting at Sheldon's old dining table. It was strange to see it there, but Sheldon loved that he and Morven had managed to mix their things until their rooms looked like they both belonged there.

Morven smiled when he heard the door and got to his feet, and Sheldon's gaze zeroed in on his stomach. He was already starting to show, and even though it flustered Morven every time Sheldon mentioned it, Sheldon thought it was adorable on such a big man. Morven was six foot six, while Sheldon was only five foot eight. Morven towered over him, and with his wide shoulders and muscles, he looked like he was always ready to step into a fight. The rounded stomach made him look softer, as did the way he behaved with it. Sheldon had noticed him stroking the skin there and even talking to the egg growing inside of him, and every time Morven did it, Sheldon lost a tiny bit of his heart to the dragon.

That was more than fine with him.

"Sorry I'm late," he said.

Morven shook his head as he stepped closer and wrapped his arms around Sheldon, pulling him against him. Sheldon could feel the curve of Morven's stomach pressing to his chest, and he smiled. He couldn't feel the baby moving since the baby was inside an egg, but it was still his son or daughter there, and his heart felt like it was about to explode with happiness.

"Don't worry about it," Morven murmured. "As long as you come back to me every evening, I don't care how late you are."

"I'm pretty sure you'll think differently once the baby is born."

Morven chuckled. "Probably. In the meantime, don't worry about it. I know you're trying to find information about the baby, and I'm grateful."

"I don't have anything yet."

Morven leaned down and kissed Sheldon's forehead. "They'll be okay. I'm sure of it. You know what the healer said. Since you managed to get me pregnant, it means that our bodies and genes are compatible. The baby will be fine."

And if they weren't, Sheldon and Morven would face that together. And they weren't alone. They'd have the support of their friends and the queen, who was ecstatic about Morven becoming a father, in more ways than one. It would add a precious baby to the clan and show everyone that dragons and humans could live together in peace.

Sheldon didn't care about any of that, though. He only cared about Morven and their baby — and their happiness.

You may also enjoy the following from eXtasy Books Inc:

Lucian had no idea what he was doing. He hadn't thought much beyond stopping and helping the man who had fallen and who, instead of getting back to his feet, had curled up and apparently waited to die. He hadn't expected Basil to do that.

He also hadn't expected Basil to be his mate.

There was no denying it. Even under the rain and the smell of gasoline coming from the road, he was sure of it. Basil was his mate, and something was wrong with him.

Lucian didn't know what to do, so he rushed to his car. He tried to be careful so they wouldn't tumble on the ground together. Whatever was wrong with his mate, he didn't want to make things worse. When he got to the car, he had a moment of hesitation. He needed to open the back door, but both his arms were around Basil. How was he supposed to do it without dropping him?

"I'm going to set you down to your feet," he told Basil. Basil's eyes were closed, and Lucian wasn't sure he was listening to him or even that he was still conscious.

"Nod if you heard me. Please, Basil. I need to put you down so I can open the door. Once you're in the car, I have a blanket for you. I'll wrap it around you, and I'll head to my brother's house. He'll be able to help you." Or at least, Lucian hoped so.

Hopefully, whatever was wrong with Basil, it was only the flu or something like that. Lucian had never heard about a shifter getting the flu, but he supposed everything was possible. Two unicorn shifters lived in Rosewood, and they should be able to heal whatever was wrong with Basil.

Lucian's knees almost buckled in relief when Basil nodded against his throat. He leaned against the car and gently lowered Basil to his feet. Basil stumbled, but since Lucian had expected it, he hadn't entirely let go. He held Basil against his body with one arm while he opened the door with the other. Once that was done, he helped lower Basil to the backseat. "You can stretch out if you want. I don't care if you get the seat wet."

Basil blinked. Now that they were in the car, Lucian could see him better. He supposed he shouldn't be surprised that he found Basil attractive. If Basil was his mate—and Lucian was sure he was—it made sense that Lucian was attracted to him.

Basil's dark wet hair hung limply down his face, and Lucian pushed it aside to see his eyes. They were open, but only to slits. Even like this, he could see that Basil had dark eyes. His skin was pale, though, too much so. It probably had a lot to do with how cold Basil was to the touch, and it made Lucian freak out a bit more. "Stay here. I'll grab the blanket."

Basil didn't even react. Lucian had to stop freaking out because he needed to get Basil to safety, and that wasn't going to happen if he couldn't think clearly.

He straightened and walked around the car, opening the trunk and moving his bags around until he found the blanket he knew was there. Once he found it, he rushed back to Basil, but Basil hadn't moved. He slumped limply against the seat, either asleep or unconscious. Probably unconscious.

"Here you go," Lucian said. He spread the blanket on top of his mate and tucked it around him so it wouldn't slip off. "I'm going to go back to the driver seat and drive you to the Rosewood pack. It's where I was going before I found you and stopped."

Lucian was pretty sure Basil couldn't hear him, but he had to continue talking on the off chance that he could. He was a nervous talker, but more importantly, he didn't want Basil to freak out. He probably hadn't expected a stranger to pick him up, and Lucian wasn't sure Basil had realized they were mates. Even he had, there was no way for him to know if Lucian wouldn't hurt him.

Not that being mates meant Lucian wouldn't. He had no idea what he was doing, but he needed to do it fast.

He closed the door once he was sure Basil was settled in as well as he could, then walked around the car. Something caught his gaze, though, and he realized it was a backpack, probably Basil's. Lucian wasted a few moments rushing to it, then carrying it to the car. Basil was going to want it once he woke up.

Because he was going to wake up.

Once he was back in the car, Lucian drove as fast as he could without crashing the car. It was still raining, and he was even wetter than he'd been before, but he didn't care anymore.

He kept peeking at the backseat, but Basil wasn't moving. Lucian was pretty sure he saw him breathing, but he couldn't have sworn to it, and he was freaking out, even though he'd told himself he wouldn't. He couldn't lose his mate, not when he'd just found him. If Basil didn't want him, that would be fine. If he died, though, it wouldn't be.

When Lucian finally reached Rosewood, he sighed in relief. He wasn't there yet, though, so he drove through the town on his way to pack territory. He knew the Rosewood pack wasn't a big one, but he still had no idea where to go once he got there. He reached for his phone, quickly dialing

Owen's number. "I need help," he said when Owen answered.

"You couldn't change the tire?"

It took Lucian a second to remember he'd had a flat tire. "I already did that, but I found a guy on the ground under the rain. He's my mate, and he's sick."

There was a moment of silence before Owen answered. "Where are you?"

"I found pack territory. I'm parking behind a house, but I don't know if it's yours. I'm going to get out of the car, grab Basil, and start walking. Please, come find me."

"I'm on my way."

Lucian didn't want to get Basil wetter and colder than he already was, but he felt he didn't have a lot of time. He turned the engine off and rushed out of the car, opening the back door and reaching for Basil. He sighed in relief when Basil murmured something and tucked himself against him the way he had earlier.

It wasn't easy to get Basil out of the car, but Lucian managed, and once he did, he hooked his arms around his mate again and hauled him up against his chest. Basil buried his face against Lucian's neck, and Lucian hoped it was a good sign. He wrapped the blanket around Basil as well as he could. It wouldn't be great protection against the rain and wind, but it was better than nothing.

He slammed the door shut with his foot, then, he started walking toward around the house. There were others, arranged in a loose circle with a fire pit in the center. Most of the houses had a light on the porch, so it wasn't as dark as it had been before. It also helped Lucian notice the men on one of the porches.

Lucian rushed toward them. At the same time, Owen and someone else—no doubt Lennox, Owen's mate—came toward him.

"We're almost there," Lucian murmured. "I'm sure my brother and his alpha will be able to help you."

"I'm dying," Basil mumbled.

"You're not. It's only a cold. I'm sure you'll be fine once we get you out of those wet clothes and warmed up."

"I'm dying," Basil repeated.

"What's going on?" Lennox asked.

Lucian's knees almost buckled in relief. "I'm not sure what's wrong with him, but I need help. He needs help." Lucian didn't care about anything else. He'd make sure Basil got everything he needed, even if he had to antagonize the Rosewood alpha — although hopefully, it wouldn't come to that.

ABOUT THE AUTHOR

Catherine is the creator of several series, most of them paranormal, including the Whitedell Pride Series and the Gillham Pack Series. While she graduated in translation, she decided to go the writer's way because it was more fun to create her own stories and characters.

She's been living in Italy for more than twenty years, but she's a daughter of the North—Belgium to be precise—and she misses it so much that she's already planning to move back.

She loves pizza—probably too much—her son, her pets, and of course, books. She sneaks some reading time into her schedule every time she has five minutes free from writing, demands from her various pets and son, and lastly, housework.

Connect with her:

lievens.catherine@gmail.com
BookBub: https://www.bookbub.com/authors/catherine-lievens
Website: https://authorcatherinelievens.com/
Facebook: https://www.facebook.com/catherine.lievens.9
Facebook Group: https://www.facebook.com/groups/411788002341528/
Twitter: https://twitter.com/authorCLievens
Newsletter: http://eepurl.com/c-uvKn

www.ingramcontent.com/pod-product-compliance
Lightning Source LLC
Chambersburg PA
CBHW060821120626
46557CB00001B/320